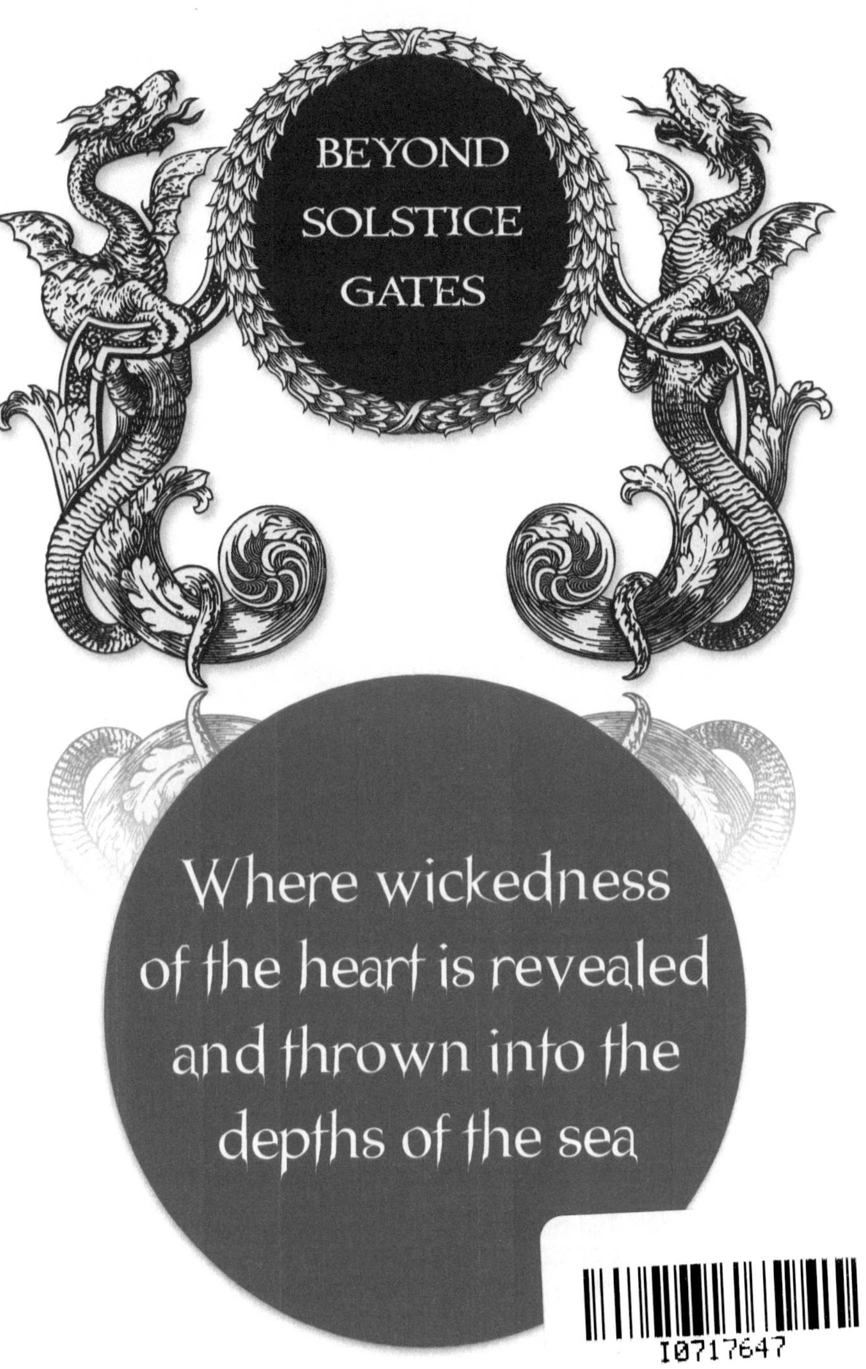

BEYOND
SOLSTICE
GATES
Where wickedness
of the heart is revealed
and thrown into the
depths of the sea
I0717647

Ahelia Publishing
Helena, Montana

MIST OVER LEVIATHAN

By Kimm Reid

BEYOND SOLSTICE GATES

Where wickedness
of the heart is revealed
and thrown into the
depths of the sea

Mist Over Leviathan

Copyright©2016 Kimm Reid

All rights reserved.
Second Edition 2018

This is a work of fiction. Names, characters, organizations, places, events, and incidents are either products of the author's imagination or are used fictitiously. No part of this book may be reproduced, scanned, or distributed in any printed or electronic form without authorized and written permission of Ahelia Publishing, LLC.

ISBN- 978-1-988001-01-2

1. Supernatural 2. Science Fiction 3. Fiction

Published in the United States of America
Printed in the United States of America

www.aheliapublishing.com
kimm.reid@outlook.com

Table of Contents

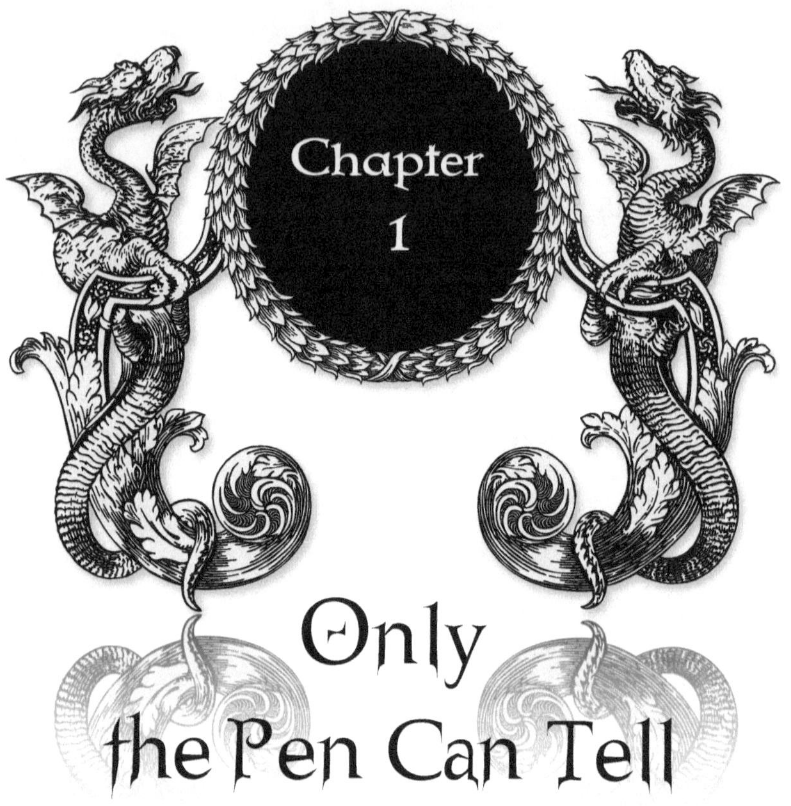

Chapter 1

Only the Pen Can Tell

The night was a long one indeed. Even though Simeon had returned Jennifer to the little yellow house on the corner of Mitchell Avenue and Fairview Lane, she was in bad shape … atrocious shape … irreparable shape, some might even say. Her hair had been singed and her fingers were raw. The Curse Breaker's body had been ravaged, but far worse than her physical wounds was the damage her heart had endured. It had been broken down, trampled over, and nearly destroyed. Seeing the shell that once held her mamma's soul had ruined Jennifer.

Bella spent the night and much of the next few days on the floor beside the rocking chair. She smoothed her niece's rough hair and gently pushed the chair back and forth when it would stop rocking. She hoped that perhaps the familiar squealing of the rocker might ease Jennifer and untwist her into some sort of comfortable peace. It was an odd hope, but Simeon had returned her to the rocker and Bella couldn't help but believe there was a good reason for that.

Judah went back and forth between the rocker and the kitchen. He sat with Bella for a while and then went to warm some milk; back to the rocker and then into the kitchen again for a muffin. It wasn't that he was particularly hungry, but he was having a difficult time just sitting there watching his shattered twin sister coiled up in the rocker; unresponsive and broken.

Every once in a while over the next few days, Judah escaped to the basement. That was his place of quietness where he spent long hours with Shemaiah. His Shailma filled him up there, in the hushed corners of the basement, with enough courage to keep going.

One foot in front of the other, my son, his Shailma would whisper to him time and time again. *Keep going ... you can do it ... trust me to shelter you. Trust Simeon to guard Jennifer. Trust is the key to believing, and if you believe, Judah,* Shemaiah would whisper, *then there is nothing you cannot do, including break the curse and release your mamma.*

After allowing his soul to be thoroughly filled by his Shailma, Judah would wander back upstairs. He prayed with every step that he'd find improvements in his sister. But as he'd step into the living room and hear the rocker, Judah would know immediately that those changes had not come. Sure, she'd stir a little, and every now and again a moan would escape from her lungs. But for a long while, that was all Jennifer could do. She had tried to open her eyes once—only once. Coming back to the reality that surrounded her was more than she could do so she hadn't bothered to try again.

Judah didn't understand that her thoughts were simply too afflicted with visions of Mamma and Justice and Tom and the others. She seemed to Bella to be asleep, and Jennifer felt she was asleep as well, although she could hear Bella and Judah and was aware of their sadness, so Jennifer knew she was not asleep at all—somewhere in the middle of asleep and awake, she supposed.

Jennifer wondered if this was what it might be like to be caught in the curse of Malleana Forest, but then as she pondered such a thing, Jennifer realized it would be far worse. Her mamma could not hear any of them, nor feel them as Jennifer was feeling Bella gently push the rocker and sweep strands of hair from her face. Her mamma was unable to hear Judah shout from the kitchen about fried eggs or warmed milk or a package from the mailman. No; the more Jennifer thought about it, the more she knew this was nothing like the forest and absolutely no comparison to what her mamma must be going through.

At about the same time the sun started to peek over the horizon on the third day, Jennifer's eyes began to flutter. Even in her half-awake-half-asleep state, she'd found comfort in the squeaky moan of the rocker. Now with her eyes open, and without moving much of herself at all, she smiled a little at the sight of both Bella and Judah hovering close. She let her eyes fall shut but before too many seconds ticked by, Jennifer opened them again—a little longer this time.

The two who had been staring at her for days began laughing as the corners of Jennifer's mouth turned up—even though it was ever so slight—for they knew then she'd be alright. A little more time dragged by before Jennifer was sitting upright sipping warm milk; Judah had heated it so many times while he waited for his sister to wake that it was quite terrible, but nobody cared. Now, looking at her and remembering the sight of his sister disappearing under the closing ground and thinking he would never see her again, this moment seemed somehow miraculously surreal and most certainly, it was.

For the first few days after Jennifer was back with them, Judah hovered and never left her side. He wanted to protect her from the slightest of things, even though he knew it was his lack of ability to protect her in Trilleah that had caused him to feel this overprotective obsession now. Nevertheless, he stayed with his sister. Even when she would be in her room—whether the door was closed or not—Judah would sit on the floor right outside the door. He vowed to never allow anything to happen to her again.

Jennifer felt unsafe regardless of how close Judah stayed and she dared not tell either him nor Bella much about what she had seen or heard that day in Trilleah … in the adder's pit. Some of the reason for keeping the secret was that she doubted they would believe her; some of the reason was that she doubted much of it herself. But the main reason Jennifer chose to keep what had happened in that adder's pit to herself was that she did not want to remember it.

She knew if she began speaking of it, both Judah and Bella would ask endless questions and return to the subject far too often. If Jennifer told them she'd heard Mamma screaming, or that she had seen the king grab her mamma, it would be unbearable. In fact, Jennifer worked hard to forget what she'd witnessed during those long moments in the adder's pit.

One day shortly after she had woken, the day after having her hair trimmed and having to watch—teary-eyed— the singed chunks fall to the floor, Jennifer found an old scribbler and wrote down everything she could recall from that dreadful place below the ground of Trilleah. Every detail her mind could find, she painstakingly jotted down—not that she hoped ever to return to the scribbler and remember, but something was nagging in her belly for her to write it down, so she did.

"Maybe if I put you on paper," she said to the words as they flowed from the tip of the pen, "I can erase you from my mind." She tried to forget. Oh, how fiercely she tried to forget.

Whenever either Judah or Bella would ask about it, Jennifer would reply with, "I cannot say," and change the subject. Often Judah and Bella would hide away in a corner somewhere and discuss how horrible it must have been and make up endless lists of what unbearable possibilities the adder's pit must have held. They knew it was terrible because it had changed Jennifer ... drastically. Whatever she had witnessed or heard or experienced in her time beneath Trilleah had changed the sweet girl. The old Jennifer was gone.

But then again, since their return from Trilleah, neither Judah nor Jennifer was the same. Their souls had been reshaped. Sure, they had fun at the local swimming pool. Often, Judah snapped his sister with the kitchen towel, or Jennifer complained about Judah's terrible table manners just as they had always done before, but there was no doubt that something was drastically different.

The rest of the summer passed quickly. The three of them sat for long stretches of time drinking cold lemonade and telling stories from the last journey; what they had seen or overheard. Trilleah had overtaken them and now, here in Westlock, their thoughts were there, in Trilleah. Judah told Jennifer about the little green jar and the words it had spoken, although he didn't mention to either of the girls he'd accidentally brought it home and had it stashed in the bottom of his dresser.

Jennifer never tried to speak of Miriam's true identity—she knew the wicked Reptilian Mindbender had put a curse on her so that she would be unable to speak of it. Nevertheless, she did try time after time to explain the adder's pit into which she was pulled; never, though, did she mention that she saw Mamma or how the others had called to her. She never told of the red dragons or how the king had taken Mamma. What she did try to explain was how Simeon had pulled her out of the dragon's nest just as she pounced onto the clay tablet. Jennifer often tried to speak of how the vines were alive and breathing; how they had held her and pulled her below the ground. She tried to make sense for them of how there was another land entirely, beneath the dirt of Trilleah.

She knew her explanations were inaccurate, but she didn't know the right words to describe such things. Perhaps those words didn't exist. Whether they did or didn't, Jennifer eventually stopped searching for them.

Regardless of the stories they shared back and forth, and no matter how many times Bella and Judah tried to reassure Jennifer that they would never allow such a monstrosity to happen to her again, Jennifer knew that neither of them had the power to control such things. No matter what they said, or how hard they tried to convince her, or how often they reminded her, Jennifer knew she had a necessary place on the journeys to the Dark Land. She knew she would return and she knew that somehow, no matter what, Simeon would be with her.

Jennifer didn't know how she knew such things for nobody had told her of them; she just knew in her heart. Simeon was the one who had rescued her. It was him who'd kept her safe and who had taught her about the laws of the land and her job there. When either Judah or Bella started in on another speech about how they had failed her and how they vowed never to fail her again, Jennifer would just nod and smile. She knew the truth, after all, even if they didn't.

The truth was that she HAD to go to that place below Trilleah; there was a tablet there. She was aware that nothing could happen unless Simeon allowed it. She had seen with her own eyes that the king couldn't come near her when Simeon refused to allow it. Jennifer knew that whatever came, it first had to come through her Shailma. If he allowed a horrible thing to come, he would also be with her and protect her … somehow. Such things were beyond her ability to understand, but Simeon had taught her that it wasn't her place to understand such things; only to trust her Shailma.

Judah and Bella hadn't expected to see Jennifer ever again, but when they'd heard the squeal of the rocking chair start singing the night of their return, they knew Simeon had brought her home. They both had run to the living room, of course, and jumped around like fools. But when they saw Jennifer, her burnt hair and her bloodied fingers which were clinging hard to the clay tablet, they both fell to the floor in front of her, unable to believe what they were seeing.

How could such a thing be? That their Jennifer had not only survived such a horrible place but had returned home with the tablet? It seemed unbelievable yet there she was; the tablet held tightly by the torn fingers of the unconscious girl. Jennifer was barely recognizable to them that morning and both Bella and Judah struggled to erase the memory of that moment.

Bella had promptly put the tablet in a glass jar on a very high shelf in the kitchen for safe keeping, but every now and again, Jennifer would climb onto the counter and take it down. She'd take it out of the jar and turn it over and over in her hands, letting her fingers drag over it, tracing the strange letters and symbols.

I wonder what they mean, she thought. *I wonder if anyone knows what they mean. I wonder how we can break the Trows' curse if nobody knows what these symbols mean.*

But as she would wonder, peace would fill up her heart and she would stop wondering and start believing. Not believing in what was uncertain, just believing in truth she didn't yet know, she supposed.

When the first snowfall came early in November, there were both shrieks of excitement as well as sighs of disappointment. While Judah loved the winters in Westlock and all the snow that came with it, both Jennifer and Bella disliked the season, and the cold, very much. There was snow to shovel off the walk, and the garden—the most beloved place of all in their quiet little town—would be put to sleep under a thick blanket of snow.

The flowers died, the grass withered, and all the wonderful trees that surrounded the yard shed their summer coat leaving only naked, ugly, dead branches. Winter was no fun, no fun at all.

In the midst of the groans and sighs of that first chilly snowfall, Bella announced that she had arranged for a small holiday for the three of them. Since they'd not be heading to Trilleah for Winter Solstice this year, they had plenty of time with no concerns or fears of the upcoming journey. Bella thought they would take a trip of their own; one filled with fun and mischief ... free from any dark things whatsoever. She thought it would do them all some good.

The twins would be turning fourteen this winter, so rather than having a big party like last year, Bella planned to take them on an adventure—one that held no Dark Lands or adder's pits. It would be an expedition where no cloaks were required, nor strange, powerful juices to be drunk ... and where no dreadful moaning could be heard. Bella was thoroughly excited about the fun she had planned, free from Living Maps and little green jars and ... Miriam.

Yes, it was going to be a wonderful adventure indeed ... eventually.

Chapter 2

When Sleep Hides

Jennifer had a hard time sleeping these days, and it was causing her to feel like she was wearing out. No matter whether it was in the dead of night or an after-school nap, the poor girl couldn't seem to find rest. It was beginning to show in her school work as well. The previous year, Jennifer had received the best grades in the class. She'd always been good in school, and since her parents' accident, much to everyone's surprise, her grades barely slipped at all.

She had decided shortly after the crash that her mamma and daddy would want her to do her best, so that is exactly what she had done. Besides, pouring herself into homework and school projects gave her something else to put her mind on. But now, with such short amounts of sleep, her best was not that great. Jennifer tried to sleep but the harder she tried, the more difficult sleep was to find.

It seemed that every time she closed her eyes, she saw her mother—not the beautiful, funny, sweet mamma she used to know, either. Jennifer would have loved for that picture to swirl and float around her mind, but that mamma was long gone. Instead, the mamma who showed up regularly behind her closed eyes was a mere shell of the woman she once knew—the one she'd seen in the adder's pit.

Jennifer thought it quite odd—when she let herself think about it, that is—that just before their last trip to the Dark Land, it was Bella who'd had the dreams about Mamma, but it was she who had seen her in the adder's pit. Jennifer recalled many times how Bella had told her and Judah about the terrible dreams on the morning they were taken to Trilleah. She still thought Bella had given the twins way too much information, even though Jennifer now knew it was all to prepare her for what she'd find in the king's lair.

Jennifer remembered little details, although she knew Bella hadn't told the twins such secrets about her dreams. Oddly, Jennifer could probably tell Bella the dreams precisely, since those vines had seemingly sucked her right into the middle of the nightmare. Yes; that's what the adder's pit was—a nightmare—Bella's nightmare.

Jennifer had a feeling that how she saw her mamma was eerily similar to how Bella had described her in the dreams—or nightmares—

yet it seemed strange to Jennifer that Bella had seen in her sleep what Jennifer saw while awake. It made her wonder if what Bella had seen was, in fact, a dream—or if her mamma somehow came to her auntie while she slept. Who could know the answers, though, to such perilous questions? So many questions without any answers—it was exhausting.

Regardless of how eerie it was or whether there were answers or no answers, Jennifer had seen Mamma. The very thing she'd prayed for night after night and hoped for day in and day out, and wished for with every falling star and birthday candle she blew out, had come to be. That very thing that she had longed for, hovered and haunted her deeply whether she was awake or searching for sleep. Jennifer couldn't escape it.

The winter was seeming long without a trip to Trilleah. Even though none of them wished to return, they did want to break the curse, no matter what. That could not be done without several trips to the Dark Land and so, not returning this particular winter seemed nearly unbearable. It felt to each of them as though time was being wasted. They spoke of it often, and every time frustration would creep in and cause them to be unsettled and … well … grouchy.

"Surely there's enough time to find another clay tablet," one would say.

"I would think the Shailmas could help us make the journey," another would add.

Before long, the annoyance would snowball into an argument and usually, when this happened they would each go to their own rooms or just stomp off. They weren't angry with each other, just annoyed beyond reason with the entire situation.

Now, with their supper half-eaten and the same frustrating conversation stirring itself up, Bella raised her voice and talked above the others.

"OK," she announced. "We shall not talk about Trilleah or anything of it until it's time for us to return at Summer Solstice," she commanded. "And Judah," she added with her voice still sounding annoyingly commanding, "pass the bread."

"But Aunt Bella ..." Judah protested. He had now thought himself too grown up to call her auntie any longer. "Does that mean we mustn't speak of Mamma either?"

"Oh dear boy, of course not!" Bella chuckled and looked horrified at the same time. "We would NEVER, not speak of Molly and Theo and remember her and ..."

"But Auntie," Jennifer interrupted, "we cannot speak of Mamma without speaking of Trilleah." She grabbed a piece of the bread as it went by and dipped it straightaway into the gravy that had pooled in the middle of her plate.

Bread—especially these warm, thick slices of French bread— was a treat these days. Bella's hours at the library had been cut back, and winter had come early this year, freezing out much of her vegetable garden that she'd normally take and sell at the farmer's market. Money had become scarce and with such a cold winter, they had to be more careful with everything. It only managed to make winter longer, colder, and more miserable—if such a thing were possible.

"We could just remember the good things Mamma used to do around here," Judah suggested.

"Maybe tell stories of when we were little!" Jennifer added.

"Good ideas; both of you," Bella said, trying to sound excited. Deep down, though, they all knew that any talk of Mamma—no matter how hard they might try—would lead to how they missed her terribly and how vile the Trows were for stealing her soul. This would, of course, lead to the topic of Trilleah where Jennifer would be reminded of what her eyes had seen in the wretched adder's pit below the vineyard.

The poor dear, already thin and frail, would again become unable to eat. Both Bella and Judah were concerned for her health and if this was to continue throughout the winter, they weren't sure what they'd do with her.

Oh, why could they not go to Trilleah for Winter Solstice? It was coming quickly; next week in fact! Even though they would have dreaded the trip, at least they might have felt like they were doing something about the curse ... and the king! They could have looked forward to finding a tablet and being one step closer to freeing the souls of the Waiting Ones—and Mamma—even if they dreaded their time in the Dark Land.

But this time, it was not to be. The decision had been taken out of their hands. If their Shailmas did not come for them, they simply couldn't get there, and the Shailmas had already made it clear they would not be returning until Summer Solstice.

"OK then," Bella announced. "It's settled. The only talk of Molly and Theo will be to remember the wonderful things that have gone on here. No more talk of that Dark Land, or its dreadful king, or anything else of that miserable place."

"Fine," Judah said.

"OK," Jennifer whined.

They all knew it wouldn't last, for this was not the first time this conversation had been had. Oh, it would work for awhile, and a while was all they could hope for.

As they finished their supper in silence—except for a hiccup here or slurp there—Simeon came momentarily to Jennifer.

Little One, he whispered to her mind, *don't fret*. Then he said something Jennifer had never considered before—something she wished she would not have to consider now because she had no idea how to consider such a thing.

Your mamma is not alone in Trilleah. She, too, has a Shailma, and he is with her there. Even though she cannot hear him right now, her Shailma is there. Your mamma is not alone.

At first, that seemed to bring an enormous amount of comfort to Jennifer. She continued to drag chunks of bread through the warm, salty gravy. It was by far one of her favorite tastes. She wondered about this new piece of information from Simeon all the while but said nothing to the others. As days went by, in fact, she said less and less about anything to the others. It seemed she needed time to get lost in her thoughts and furthermore, she'd been spending more time having deep conversations with Simeon, learning, trying to understand things far beyond her ability to do so.

The rest of this particular evening, Jennifer was quieter than usual, which was unsettling to Bella. Jennifer knew it but made no effort to change it for Bella's sake. She couldn't help but ponder this new idea that Simeon had recently deposited into her thoughts. Did Mamma have a Shailma of her own? But why? Why did she need a Shailma? How was this even possible? Could it be so? Maybe she had heard Simeon wrong! Yes ... that must be it. She must have heard him wrong.

Jennifer tried to put all the rambling thoughts out of her mind —for awhile—all the way back to the farthest corner of her mind but she couldn't. They just lingered, waiting to be thought about, waiting to be asked about, waiting to be given attention.

The three of them tried to play a board game after supper had been cleaned up—just to pass the time—but eventually it was put away without being finished. This wasn't the first time this winter that a game would not be played to the end. Jennifer couldn't concentrate; her mind was far from the dotted dice or her red game pieces or the cards she was supposed to pay attention to. Her mind was not even in Trilleah, where both her brother and her auntie assumed it would be.

No; her mind was on the Shailmas. Jennifer suddenly had a pile of questions that she realized she'd never considered before now. Like a giant ball of yarn that had been wrapped up tightly, she suddenly had a great need to unwrap it and think all the things her mind had failed to think before now; things that had been wound up firmly in the thoughts and ponderings that they'd not had a chance to be considered or pondered—until now.

"Maybe we'll play later," Bella finally said after much huffing and grumbling from Judah.

Typically when Jennifer would become distracted and Bella would say such a thing, Jennifer would become aware of her distractedness. She'd shake her head and try harder to focus. But not tonight. Tonight she said, "Yes, let's," and wandered away—straight to the rocker without putting her game pieces back in the box.

Since Simeon had returned her to the rocker that dreadful night a few months ago, it had become Jennifer's favorite place to think and find her Shailma. She would let the squeaking dull her mind to the point of being able to focus completely on what was going on inside of it. Jennifer was able to shut out everything in the living room … and the house … and the winter … and Westlock … and dwell on whatever it was she wanted to dwell on.

Tonight it was the Shailmas her mind focused on; more specifically, the confusing thoughts that Simeon had just given her—about her mamma having a Shailma who stayed with her even though she was caught in the curse of Malleana Forest.

Judah noticed the rocker was where she headed now and he poked Bella.

"There she goes again," he whispered.

"Oh dear," Bella sighed and stopped putting game pieces into the box. "I wish she'd talk about what happened in that adder's pit."

"She'd feel better; I'm sure she would," Judah replied. Neither of them understood that what Jennifer had seen and heard and smelled and felt in the grip of that pit was far too dreadful to merely be "talked about."

Jennifer had wanted to speak of it, to tell them about it, and many times she'd tried to form the words in her mind. Each time, though, she was reminded that there were no words to describe any of it, so she wouldn't even try.

This was not where her mind went tonight, however. Tonight, her mind was completely turned over and over and over the comment from Simeon. If Mamma was not alone because she had a Shailma, why did the Shailma allow her soul to be stolen in the first place? Could the Shailma not have stopped such a thing? Were the Shailmas unable to comfort her mamma or why was she wailing such a dreadfully painful wail? It was that horrible sound that Jennifer could not banish from her ears even now, months later. That wretched sound brought pain to her head every time she remembered it—and she remembered it often.

What Simeon had meant to bring comfort to Jennifer, brought no comfort whatsoever. It brought many things, but comfort was not among them. It brought questions. It brought fear. It brought anger. It caused the trust in her own Shailma to waiver a little.

If Mamma's Shailma could not protect her soul from the Trows, how would Jennifer ever be able to trust that Simeon could protect her soul? If Mamma's Shailma—if in fact, she did have one—was with her, why was Mamma so wretched and why couldn't he rescue her from the curse that held her there? Had the Shailma failed? If Mamma's Shailma failed so dreadfully, then couldn't her own Shailma fail as well?

Why, Simeon? she asked over and over again. *Why?*

The singing that was sent out from the rocker's squeak lulled Jennifer's mind and carried it far away from her surroundings and far away from the wondering eyes of her auntie and brother. She knew they were watching her. They were always watching her. She didn't care; let them watch.

Maybe if they watched her so closely here, they would watch her more carefully in Trilleah and the land would have no opportunity to do again what it had successfully done before.

"I worry about her, Judah," Bella sighed.

"I know," he replied sullenly. "So do I."

Secrets in Ink

Such was the way things went night after night in the Elliot house. Bella tried her best to preoccupy the twins and keep their minds off of what had occurred in Trilleah a few months earlier. She'd sometimes try to set up a board game, but Jennifer would soon lose interest, or her mind would wander too far to come back when it was her turn. Bella would try and plan trips to the theater or the swimming pool or even to Martha's Maltz ... but both Judah and Jennifer would refuse to go.

Bella had the twins' friends over in an attempt to distract them, but that failed every time. No matter what she tried, Bella had been unsuccessful in her efforts to keep the twins preoccupied and distracted.

Ever since that moment in the Dark Land where Judah looked into his sister's eyes as the ground closed between them, he refused to let her out of his sight; even in school. Most years the twins requested to be in different classes, but not this year. This year, Judah demanded to be in the same class as Jennifer and even arranged to sit right behind her. Bella was surprised that Jennifer didn't get annoyed with him, but then again, Jennifer was so preoccupied most of the time, perhaps she never even noticed her brother's continual hovering.

Regardless, Bella was confident that her biggest plan yet would work to get the twins' minds off of Trilleah and off of that one dreadful moment. She was sure Jennifer would finally come out of her mind which had ensnared her for months. Bella was excited about the whole thing and it couldn't come soon enough.

Auntie Bella had good reason to wish for the plan to hurry, for the twins' fourteenth birthday was coming up soon and this was sure to bring up some unrest—not unrest due to the twins' birthdays, but unrest because it was the same day as Winter Solstice. The Shailmas had made it clear they would not be coming for their Travelers this particular Solstice because of the shortness of the day and the danger of running out of sunlight in Trilleah. It seemed none of the Shailmas were willing to put their Travelers at risk of being caught in the Dark Land and instead, decided to wait until Summer Solstice.

The remaining clay tablets would take every possible second of daylight in the Summer Solstices; the Winter Solstices would be useless to the Travelers from now on—or so said the Shailmas.

Because of this, Bella was concerned about the day. She fretted about how the twins would respond to the day. After all, it had been a while now since their birthdays had not held something enormous. Their parents' accident had occurred on their birthday and then, only two years later, Jennifer had begun traveling to Trilleah. Judah started visiting the land even before that!

Yes, Bella was worried; she had good reason to be.

That is why, months earlier, she'd planned a trip for their birthdays. You see, when they had all left Trilleah in the summer, none thought Jennifer would survive. When Simeon had returned her to their little yellow house—when he had brought her back to that annoying rocking chair—Bella made sure to let the others know; at least the others whom she could contact.

She had no way of contacting Kaija Mae since she remained in the Dark Land, nor did she have any way of contacting Aviel, Tahlia, or the others who stayed behind. Of course, it goes without saying that Miriam had not been informed. Bella had no knowledge of how to contact her and even if she could, she wouldn't have. It seemed best if Miriam had as little information as possible—especially about Jennifer.

All the other Travelers, though, were excited and wanted to see that little one who they thought they'd never see again. They'd have been satisfied to wait until Winter Solstice, but because they were not gathering in Asphelia's Hollow on that day, it seemed too long to wait until Summer Solstice; a whole year seemed an unbearably long time to wait to reunite with Jennifer.

Bella had worked hard and finally forged a perfect plan. Oh, the twins were going to be so surprised. Bella and the twins would head west while Matt and Pierce would come east, meeting them in the middle. Sam lived quite close to where they were meeting and he was, of course, extravagantly excited. It would be a long drive, but it was going to be worth it; Bella was sure of that.

Matt's family, it turned out, was very wealthy and had a large cabin beside a beautiful lake. There were all sorts of great things to do and lots of room for everyone. It was going to be quite a surprise, one with fun and laughing and plenty of sun for the twins—and everyone else—to enjoy. Bella crossed her fingers and hoped it would be well worth the sacrifice it was going to take for her to pull it off.

With having so little as it was, saving for such a trip had proven to be a tough task for the young auntie. Bella wasn't working at the library much these days but had managed to do some odd jobs around town—like cleaning for a few seniors as well as doing some cooking for a large church event that fall.

The twins knew nothing about it other than they were going somewhere for about six days, and to pack for warm sunny days and chilly nights. Judah and Jennifer were intrigued and spent a good while trying to figure out Bella's plan. It turned out that their auntie could be very tight-lipped when she chose to be.

Jennifer didn't particularly want to go anywhere, but Bella was confident that when her niece saw Matt, her attitude would shift quickly.

Sure, the warm sun part sounded tempting, but Jennifer was lazy and would have been perfectly happy (as happy as she could be, that is) curled up in front of the fireplace with a mug of hot cocoa and a good book. Of course, Jennifer never wished to go too far from home. Bella had thought it was just because she was very busy being a grump, but Judah knew differently.

His sister confided in him more than Bella ever knew, so Judah was well aware that Jennifer wanted to remain close to home just in case Simeon changed his mind and decided to come for her. She was worried that he wouldn't know where to find her if she was not in the little yellow house on 123 Fairview Lane.

Judah insisted that Simeon must be like Santa Claus! No matter where she was, both the Shailma and Santa would always find her. While Judah meant it to be funny and bring a smile to his sister's sad face, it had not. It only brought more despair.

"Oh, Jelly Bean," he said with a sigh. "It will be fine … it will all be fine … I promise you."

Jennifer didn't respond because unlike last winter at this time, she sincerely doubted it would be fine. She doubted that anything would ever be fine again. She thought briefly about trying to explain to her brother a few things she'd seen and heard in the adder's pit, but decided against even trying and so, she never did.

Instead, she continued to write in the scribbler she'd found in her desk drawer a few days back with only a few pages used. She had ripped those pages out and began using that scribbler to write down all the things she'd seen and experienced in Trilleah. Right from the beginning, as far back as she could remember from her very first journey, she continued to write it all down; every detail became etched onto those pages.

The scribbler was getting full, but there was still some room for more. The dreaded trip to the adder's pit had been jotted down along with this thing and that memory. Most recently, she had added things about Mamma. Jennifer wrote all about how she had heard the familiar voice calling to her and how she watched as the king's dragon-like creature refused to move toward her because of the circle of Shamar Shailmas surrounding her. Through watery eyes, Jennifer detailed on the pages of her scribbler precisely how she'd heard the voices and then had seen the empty shells of the loved ones of her friends—Matt's father, Tom … Sam's little sister, Justice … and Peter. She described them in as much detail as her soul would allow.

It all seemed to be too much, but as she wrote it down. It somehow became more bearable; lighter maybe. It was as though when the visions and words and memories found a place in the scribbler, they were released from her mind. They became less heavy, and so she wrote more. More and more and more she penned into that tattered scribbler, freeing up bigger and bigger spaces in her mind. As she continued writing, Jennifer became more peaceful and less sad. Both Judah and Bella began noticing the changes, and although small, it gave them some hope—equally small, but there nevertheless.

Jennifer was always careful to hide her scribbler. It had quickly become all the thoughts in her mind—fully exposed on paper for any eyes to see. Between those two covers, her deepest thoughts were cradled—her most horrible memories, and her biggest fears. It scared her a little to think that one day she might forget to hide the scribbler and have either Judah or Bella discover it.

Even though she had written in thick black marker across the cover, **STAY OUT! PRIVATE!** Jennifer knew full well that if either of them found the scribbler, they would most certainly *not* stay out.

This evening, as Jennifer sat on the floor of her room tucked between her bed and the dresser, she furiously wrote in the scribbler. Thoughts were flooding her mind tonight—more memories of the adder's pit mostly—and she jotted them down. Jennifer was afraid to miss even the tiniest detail so she wrote quickly. Once her mind was cleared out, she went right back to wondering about the Shailmas.

"Simeon," she said aloud. "Help me understand."

Almost instantly, she heard Simeon's voice loud and clear; not in her mind, but with her ears. His audible voice was not heard often outside of Trilleah, so she was startled but listened carefully.

"Oh, dear Jennifer, a storm—no matter how terrible—never means that the Shailmas have left. The presence of the storm never implies the absence of the Shailma; it only means the Shailma can't be seen because the eyes of the one who's looking are on the storm."

Jennifer began to interrupt, as was her usual habit, but this time Simeon would not have it and he kept right on speaking. "Little One, you have been in storms. Just a few days ago there was a terrible snow storm right here in Westlock. You were able to miss school because of it; do you recall?"

"Yes, I remember," she answered.

"Could you see the houses across the street?" Simeon asked, waiting patiently for the girl to wander back in her memories and find the answer. He didn't wait long since Jennifer knew exactly what he was speaking about. She and Judah had been looking out the window facing the street, watching the snow come down so heavy and blow so hard that she had pointed out their inability to see the houses across the street.

"No, I couldn't see them," she said sheepishly.

"OK," Simeon said, "You couldn't see the houses, but did that mean the houses were no longer there?"

"Of course not," Jennifer almost giggled at such a ridiculous thought, but she hadn't giggled since her time in the adder's pit; she wasn't about to start now.

"That's how it is with Shailmas, Little One." Simeon waited to see if Jennifer would get it on her own, but then he continued. "You cannot see in a storm."

In an instant she got it, and she smiled.

"Mamma's in a storm," she whispered more to herself than to Simeon. As though a lightbulb came on in her mind, it suddenly made sense. She enjoyed these moments when Simeon would awaken her mind to things, but as she thought about how much sense this thing made, it caused her to wonder what other things that made no sense to her troubled mind were as simple as this.

"Oh, how I would like to understand everything," she sighed.

"And one day you will, Little One," Simeon whispered back to her. "One day you will."

Chapter 4

Misery of Memory

For tonight, the sun had found its place somewhere behind the horizon and the day was finally put to bed. Jennifer pulled herself from the cozy little corner she'd tucked herself into and stretched her legs. They were stiff, and when she looked over at the clock she knew why. The girl had been sitting for a long time—much longer than she'd even realized! Jennifer sighed loudly, although nobody was around to hear her. The time had passed so quickly, as it always did when she was discussing things with her Shailma, and tonight it annoyed her for some reason.

Jennifer was perfectly aware that having such deep conversations with a Shailma was an unusual experience. Each time—without exception—those conversations which seemed to last only a very few moments turned out to take up much more time than it had seemed. That passing time was never fully realized until Jennifer would look at the clock. She'd always end up wondering where the time went during those conversations.

Tonight was no different. As Jennifer tucked her scribbler into its usual hiding spot under the corner of her mattress and climbed into bed, she realized it was quiet on the other side of the door. The tired girl grabbed her tattered red blanket and began her usual sleep ritual of winding the tassels around her fingers and letting them loosen and fall off. Again and again she did this, night after night, and the blanket was worn through.

As she was somewhat comforted by the blanket, Jennifer began to think. It made sense that both Bella and Judah had gone to bed since it was after midnight, but it seemed odd that neither stopped in to say goodnight or check on her. They always checked on her. In fact, they checked on her so much it was becoming annoying.

She knew those two were ferociously worried about her, and it made her feel good ... most of the time. Nevertheless, there were occasions—though not many—where she wanted nothing other than to be left alone, but there one of them would always be, peeking at her or knocking on her door or watching her from across the room.

"Oh well," she said to the air. Jennifer couldn't blame either of them. She couldn't imagine how she might feel if she thought Judah would be gone forever. The look in his eyes as the ground closed over her in the adder's pit was nearly unbearable. Trying to glance through Judah's eyes and see what he saw was far too much for her to consider.

Regardless, Jennifer snuck out of bed and quietly pulled her door open. She tossed the blanket back toward the bed and stuck her head into the hallway. She looked this way and that and then, seeing nobody, she snuck to the kitchen for some warm milk and to make sure everything was the way it was supposed to be. Her bedroom light was still on; she rarely turned it off these days. Too many unknowable things wanted to hide in the darkness it seemed, and unlike Trilleah, she could control the darkness at home with the flip of a switch—so she did. Bella never complained about the light being on all the time.

Jennifer was not in the kitchen for even five minutes before Judah was there too. She thought she'd been very quiet, but when her brother stuck his nose into the kitchen she wondered if she'd woken him or if he was just waiting to hear any sound she might make so he'd have an excuse to get up and spy on her. Jennifer didn't mind the reason; she was glad he was here with her.

"I'll have some of that, Jelly Bean," he whispered as he entered the kitchen.

"Did I wake you?" she whispered back and poured more milk into the pot on the stove.

"I wasn't sleeping," he said. "I have trouble sleeping lately."

"Judah," she said while continuing to stir the milk. "Do you think Mamma and Daddy have Shailmas?"

A rather odd question to come so late in the night, don't you think? Judah wondered to himself. It was a thought too heavy for him to think about right now, so he just shrugged his shoulders.

"I dunno," he sighed. "Never really thought much about it. Besides, it doesn't matter now whether they do or they don't. Where they are right now, I don't think either Mamma or Daddy would have much use for a Shailma."

"I suppose not," she muttered and dropped the conversation, though it did not leave her mind. She kept stirring the milk like her mamma had taught her. Judah was quiet but remained close. As she stirred and watched the white, steaming liquid swirl around and around, Jennifer became transfixed with her thoughts.

Suddenly, an idea—more of a knowing, really—came to her and as she looked up from the milk, the big spoon dropped, startling Judah. He jumped because his thoughts had taken him away from the kitchen, even though his body remained there, leaning against the doorway.

"Yes," she announced. "Of course!"

Her mind flooded with a recollection of the Shailmas that had stood enormous and surrounding her in the adder's pit. She somehow knew, without being told, that those Shailmas belonged to her mamma, and her friends' loved ones, and the others who were caught in the curse of the Trows. She was so excited at such an understanding that she forgot Judah was watching her.

"Of course, what?" he asked. This time it was he who startled her. Now Jennifer was in a predicament. Should she tell Judah what that, "of course" comment was really about? Or would it be better for her to make something up, or perhaps not answer him at all?

She bent down and picked up the big spoon, turning off the heat under the milk. Judah grabbed mugs from the cupboard.

"Of course what, Jennifer?" he asked again. Clearly, her brother wasn't going to let the words pass by unnoticed, so with only the slightest bit of pondering, Jennifer decided to tell him the truth. If he wanted to know things so badly, she would tell him. Maybe it would encourage him to mind his own business next time.

Jennifer carefully poured the steaming milk into mugs and set the pot in the sink to cool. She pulled up the tap to send some water into the pot and watched as scalding steam rose and sizzled. She grabbed her mug, turned, and wandered into the living room.

Judah rolled his eyes and tried to muster up some much-needed patience. He followed her into the living room and as she plopped down into the rocker, Judah sprawled onto the couch. Both twins pulled thick blankets over themselves. It seemed clear that they both intended to be there awhile.

"Judah, I'm going to tell you something I saw in the adder's pit that just now made sense to me." Judah instantly sat upright and even though he was trying to act calm, Jennifer knew he was listening intently. She rarely spoke of the adder's pit, and even though both he and Bella had asked countless questions and tried to push her to talk about it, she rarely did.

Judah knew he was about to be given some insight into what was going on with his sister, so he listened closely.

She opened her mouth to begin her explanation but then closed it again as she realized she had no idea where to start. The beginning was a long way back. Her mouth started moving ever so slightly, but no sounds were coming out. Judah realized she must be talking to her Shailma.

He didn't want to interrupt for fear she'd get annoyed and not say anything more about the adder's pit or what she'd just realized about it. But he did want to know what happened there and what she'd seen and experienced, so he waited—with very little patience—but he waited all the same.

Finally, and with the milk mostly drunk, her words began spilling from her mouth, filling up the air between the twins. Some of her words made sense to Judah and others made no sense at all. He listened intently, nevertheless.

Jennifer told of how she had seen the king in the adder's pit, since that disgusting place was his throne room. "Why any king would choose an adder's pit for a throne room is beyond me," she muttered. "But then again, I suppose when you're a king of the serpents, it would be perfect. Yes," she muttered to herself. "That must be right."

Jennifer recalled how the king had seen her, even though she had tried to hide, and how his black eyes stared straight into her own.

"I closed my eyes because I didn't want him to see into my soul but then," and for a moment, as she pondered her thoughts carefully, she was quiet. "But then I became so afraid because I couldn't see him, that I had to open them again. I didn't want to."

Jennifer took another moment to gather her breath because as she remembered the king staring through her eyes and into her soul, all of her breath got caught somewhere in-between here and there.

"That detestable king tried to come at me, but the beast he was on refused to move." She remembered out loud how the king smashed his metal boots into the beast's belly, slicing it thoroughly and demanding the creature to move … but it wouldn't budge.

Judah thought that for a moment, his sister felt poorly for this beast, but he convinced himself he was wrong. He had to be.

As Jennifer recalled more and more and more, she was reminded of this detail or that moment she'd forgotten about until now. Before long she forgot that Judah was even in the room. She rattled off her memories as they stirred in her mind. As she did, Judah sat rigid and wide-eyed—he could not believe what he was hearing.

In the worst of all movies he'd watched, he'd never seen such horridness that his sister—his small, frail sister—was telling him about now. No wonder Jennifer had changed so drastically. No wonder she was quiet and sullen most of the time. An enormous amount of pride began growing in Judah's belly over this girl who was clearly the very opposite of what he'd thought her to be. She was valiant and had a strength that left him flabbergasted. Who he saw here, was not who Jennifer was there.

Judah's eyes filled to the brim with hot tears, and for a long time he succeeded in keeping them from spilling over. But as he listened to his sister recall how she heard Mamma screaming her name and how she was a shell without her soul, Judah's tears became too many, and they rolled down his cheeks.

He reminded himself that boys are not supposed to cry—especially in front of their sisters—but he decided that he didn't care. Besides, his sister was the only other one in the room, and she had gone somewhere deep inside her mind and had forgotten he was even there.

Jennifer didn't realize she was replaying the entire story of the adder's pit out loud. Perhaps she'd kept it all locked in her mind for so long that—like Judah's tears—the thoughts had become too many and overflowed before she could stop them.

"Simeon let me see him with my eyes and he told me to look around." In her mind, she was right back there in the adder's pit, Judah could tell, which is most likely why she rarely spoke about it. He suddenly understood her quietness and was sorry for the times he had asked her and had become frustrated when she refused to speak of it.

But now, in the darkness of the night, Jennifer knew she had to let Judah know what she'd seen.

"I looked around me, Judah, and somehow I was able to see all things that were there, both in the land and in the atmosphere. All those things both seen and unseen were suddenly visible to me."

Judah had no idea what to say or how to respond to such things, so he kept quiet. He couldn't understand anything she was saying since he had never experienced anything of the sort. He wanted to encourage or console his sister but wasn't sure exactly which. Judah was afraid that if he said the wrong thing, she'd close her mouth—and her heart—for good.

He sat silently and waited without patience.

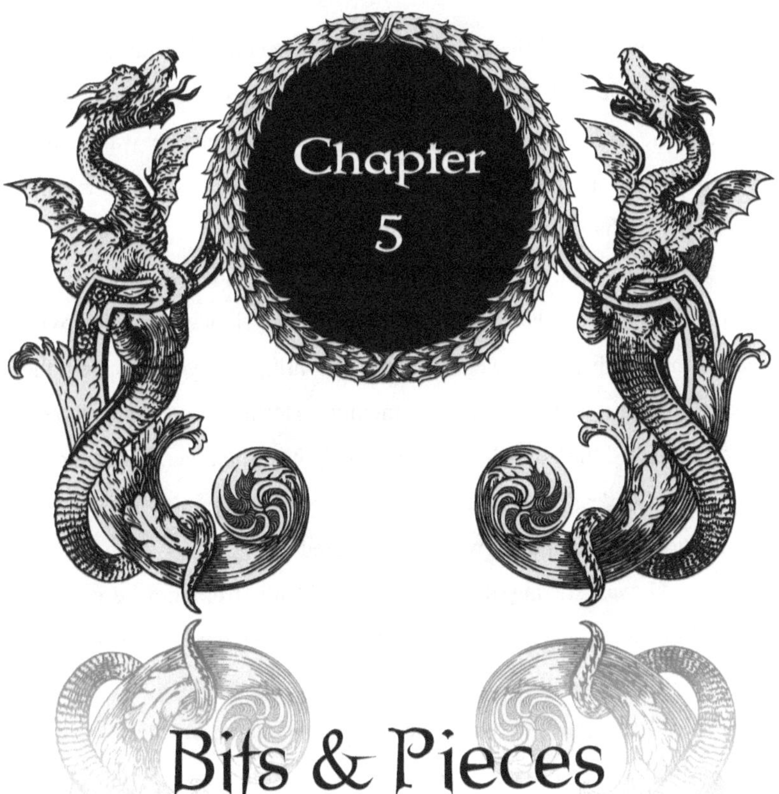

Chapter 5

Bits & Pieces

"Judah, what Simeon showed me was a wall—no, a circle—of Shailmas surrounding me. They were enormous! Ten feet tall, without any exaggeration, and they surrounded me on every side. There was no way King Shrailzhar could get to me. He either didn't see the ring of Shailmas or didn't care, but that beast he sat on saw, knew. That devil creature saw them and no amount of kicking or beating from Shrailzhar was going to cause that savage beast to move even one step closer."

She stopped there, leaving Judah speechless but not satisfied. Jennifer had started telling him about something she'd realized while stirring the milk but hadn't gotten to that part yet. He waited and watched his sister. He hoped she'd continue but was ready to remind her of that "Aha" moment if she didn't.

She didn't. After many minutes, Judah said, "Jelly Bean, was that what you suddenly realized now?" She looked at him with confusion. "When you were stirring the milk, and you dropped the spoon," he said, hoping to jar her memory. Her memory wasn't jarred. "You asked if I thought Mamma and Daddy had Shailmas?" That did it.

"Oh yes!" she suddenly became excited again as if whatever realization she'd had then, was now repeated.

"I was stirring the milk and suddenly from nowhere—well from Simeon, I suppose—I knew who those Shailmas belonged to." With that, she was off on another long, breathless explanation.

"I thought they were the Shamar Warriors, but they weren't. Up until a few minutes ago, that's who I thought they were!"

"Judah," she whispered and lowered her voice as if others were there whom she did not wish to have the information she was about to reveal to her brother. "I saw Mamma. She called to me. And there were others … many others. I heard Sammy's little sister calling me. Oh, Judah, she's so young."

Judah had an expression cover his face that he'd most certainly be embarrassed by if he could see himself. It was dumbfounded and disbelief and confusion and awe all twisted into one. He couldn't see himself, of course, so he let the awkward look remain and kept his ears tuned carefully to every word that was coming from Jennifer's lips.

"Justice has such a soft voice," Jennifer sighed. "I still hear it, Judah. Every night I hear her voice calling me."

"Who is Justice?" he asked.

"I just told you!" she huffed. "She's Sam's baby sister."

Well, she hadn't really told him *who* she was, but he could tell his question had annoyed Jennifer, and so he quickly said, "Yes, of course!" so that she would continue telling him the things he'd waited so long to hear.

"Matthew's father, Tom, also called to me. I think he must have been a very big man." She pondered some things for a few minutes without speaking about them. Judah dared not ask.

"There were many calling to me—calling my name—and then I saw one who was obviously Peter because he looked exactly like Pierce." She rambled on and on and on. "The place was so horrid, so wretched, so disgusting, that I thought I'd like to wish Pierce and Peter to change places but then realized I would not wish even Pierce to be in such a dreadful place."

"Anyway, all these shells of the not-dead-but-most-certainly-not-alive, were calling my name ... screaming it. I couldn't believe they knew my name, but they did. Judah, the reason I cannot find sleep is that I still hear them calling me ... all the time they call me to rescue them. Day and night, night and day, their screams haunt me."

She was quiet again but not for long this time.

"Judah," she whispered, "the Shailmas that were surrounding me, protecting me from the king ... they belonged to those who were caught in the curse: Mamma, Justice, Tom, Peter, and the others. Oh, there are so many others."

"Judah," she sighed and paused, for this was the point of the entire conversation, and she did not wish for her brother to miss it. She stopped rocking and shifted her eyes to look directly at her brother and waited until he looked right back at her. "Mamma has a Shailma and he is with her even in the adder's pit—even in the curse."

Judah stared at his sister. He knew he had heard the words right because he made her repeat them, but they could find no place to settle in his mind. The same questions that had been rolling in Jennifer's head earlier about this very idea now stirred in his. Jennifer found his reaction amusing and decided that was what she must look like to Simeon most of the time; confused, bewildered and frustrated.

As she sat—quite pleased with herself—watching her brother, she was surprised when his gaze suddenly moved to the kitchen. She turned around to find what had caught his attention and saw that Bella had gotten up and was now standing quietly around the corner. Neither of the twins had noticed her until now, so they had no idea how long she'd been there nor how much of the conversation she had overheard.

Not much, Jennifer hoped. *The less she heard, the better. If Bella heard too much, she might not allow me to return to Trilleah.*

It never occurred to Jennifer—perhaps because it was very late or maybe because she hadn't slept properly in months—that Bella had no say in such matters. Only Shailmas could make such decisions, but she didn't think about that now.

The twins waited for her to come into the living room and join them … or tell them to get to bed. After all, it was a school night and well after midnight. They sat quietly. Jennifer even stopped rocking in her chair to make sure the squealing was silent.

To their surprise, though, she did neither. Bella got a drink from the tap, cleared her throat, and went back down the hallway without saying a word. Maybe she didn't notice them at all.

They listened for the latch on her door to click, but it never did, so they knew she hadn't closed her door.

"Oh, good grief," Jennifer mumbled. Judah said nothing. The look on his face said he was confused and filled with questions.

Somewhere in the night, a coyote howled. "He seems awfully close to the house," Jennifer commented sleepily. She realized that she'd become quite drowsy, and groaned as she stood up. "I'm going to bed," she said, stretching her arms far above her head. Jennifer finally felt like she might be able to sleep tonight and didn't want to miss the opportunity.

"Really?" Judah finally said. "You tell me this stuff about the adder's pit and Mamma and the others and visible Shailmas and that you talked to Mamma—sorta—and now you're just going to go to bed?" He seemed unimpressed, but that was fine with Jennifer. Maybe it would be Judah who would lay awake hour after hour tonight, waiting for the sun to come up and begging sleep to find him.

"Yup," she answered. "Judah, I'm sorry if the story gets to you, but I was *there*. It's haunted me every night since, and now I'm tired." She had reached the kitchen by now and ran water into her cup. "You have asked me about it a thousand times, and now you have the information you've been looking for. Perhaps now you know why I never wanted to tell you in the first place."

"I've had plenty of time to ponder and consider and question and argue—and all the other things one can do with such information—and it's worn me out!"

That was understandable, Judah supposed. It was about the only thing that made any sense at all, so he stood and walked toward his sister. Part of him was glad to have some of the information that had been haunting her, and part of him wished he still knew nothing. All of him knew, however, that there was still much information his sister had kept to herself. If the parts she had told him were so horrid, it made him wonder even more what she wasn't telling him. He still didn't know how her hair got singed. For this night, though, he had enough of her story and asked her no more questions—not right now, at least.

In an odd and awkward manner, he leaned down and hugged his sister—who was much shorter than him now—and kissed her on the forehead.

"I am so sorry, Jelly Bean." He took her by the hand and walked her down the hallway until they reached her door. "I'm sorry I couldn't protect you from such things," he said. "I promise to do better and try harder and pay closer attention."

"Judah," she whispered in a sleepy voice, "it wasn't your fault, and you did not fail me or let me down. It had to happen. There was a tablet in the pit, and it needed to be collected. It had to be, Judah. Things work out the way they're supposed to, it seems."

With that, she squeezed his hand, darted into her room, and closed the door.

Chapter 6

Back for More

Judah had no way of calmly considering all his sister had just shared with him, but he was going to try. What did she mean, "things work out the way they're supposed to?" *She's gone mad*, he reasoned. *That's the only way any of this makes sense. She's gone mad!*

He dragged himself back to his room but left the door wide open. This was unusual for Judah because as the only boy in the house, he enjoyed his privacy. For a reason he couldn't put his finger on, tonight he felt like it should be open; wide open. "Just in case," he whispered, but just in case of what, he had no idea. Still, the door would remain open, and the hall light would stay on.

He felt odd in his insides and immediately asked his Shailma about it.

Shemaiah, he wondered, *what did Jennifer mean about things working out the way they are supposed to? Was it necessary then, that she was pulled into the adder's pit? Is that what was suppose to be? Was there nothing I could have done to stop it? I don't understand.*

The boy was getting himself quite worked up. The more he wondered, the more questions arose. The more questions arose, the more confused he became. Finally, he wondered if he knew anything at all. *It seems,* he finally huffed to his Shailma in utter frustration, *the more I learn, the more I realize that I know nothing whatsoever!*

Yes, Judah was indeed frustrated to a full measure. If he would have asked just one, or maybe even two questions, and given Shemaiah time to answer them, he'd have saved himself a load of unnecessary worry and anxiousness, but he did not. Judah asked far too many questions without waiting for answers to any of them and so, as it goes with Shailmas, he received answers to none of them.

Now, in the wee hours of the morning with the sun still sleeping behind the cold, snow-covered horizon, here he was. Tired but far from sleep; frustrated but far from answers; wondering if he had any purpose in Trilleah at all. If Judah couldn't even keep his fragile twin sister from being wrenched below the ground, what good was he? Hmm, of all things he had to consider deeply, this was the one that bothered him the most.

"Judah. Judah!"

The boy rubbed his eyes. Someone was calling him and gently shaking him. He opened one eye just a crack, for a crack was all that was needed to see Bella on the side of his bed. The instant her face connected to his eyes, he sprang up. Poor Judah had not even realized he'd fallen asleep.

Sure, he had laid down and pulled a blanket over himself, but the last thing he remembered were questions and thoughts and disappointing exaggerations of his lack of importance or necessity in Trilleah. All such things swirled and spun and twisted around in his mind. He must have dozed off while thinking of them.

Judah sat up and rubbed his head. Oh, what a headache he had. Maybe he slept crooked. He rubbed the back of his neck. No, the pain was definitely in his head. The tired boy rubbed his eyes again and then looked back to Bella, who continued to sit on the side of his bed. She hadn't spoken anything other than his name to wake him.

"Is it morning?" Judah asked.

"Oh no, Judah, it's not morning." She smiled. He cranked his head to see the clock, but Bella was blocking it from where she sat. "It is well into the afternoon. You missed the morning altogether."

"I did?" he seemed confused but then again, why wouldn't he be?

Bella scratched the boy's head with her fingernails. He'd always loved when she did that. Even as a small boy it comforted him when his mamma did it, and Bella began doing it the night of the accident to try and calm him. He was getting much too old for such things, but every once in a while, he would still allow it.

"Don't worry, Judah," she smiled. "I called the school and let them know you and J would be missing today. You needed the rest."

"Jennifer slept in too?" he asked.

"Not nearly as long as you, but yes, a little. I didn't wake her either this morning because both of you were up very late last night discussing things that greatly needed discussing." Sometimes Bella would let the twins miss a school day here and there for something other than what the school would say were "acceptable reasons."

They had always done well in school, and even though Jennifer was not doing well this year, there were perfectly reasonable explanations for it, and so Bella allowed them a day here and there. This was "one of those days," Judah assumed.

He could not have been more wrong, however, and as he laid back down, Bella pulled on his arm.

"Oh no, you don't Mister!" she giggled. "It's time to get up." Bella stood up and walked toward the door. Just before she stepped into the hallway, she stopped and turned back to him. "Besides, you have a guest in the kitchen." And with that, she stepped into the hallway.

"Who?" Judah hollered. No answer came.

"Who is it, Aunt Bella?" She stuck her nose back around the corner and with a smirk said, "I guess you'll have to get up and come find out." Then she was gone.

He flopped himself back to his pillow and rubbed his head; it was pounding by now. *Who in the world would be here to see me?* Nobody came to his mind, not even one person. They had no grandparents who popped in now and again to surprise the twins, and all his friends would be in school. "Hmm," he pondered.

Get up, Judah, go to your visitor because there is valuable information being brought to you this day. Go now, don't delay, wafted the clear voice of Shemaiah into Judah's mind. He was rather startled but then again, not nearly as much as he thought he should be. The voice of his Shailma had become so familiar to him that he knew it, recognized it, and obeyed it. He had learned that obeying one's Shailma promised safety, wisdom, and peace—ignoring the voice brought the opposite.

He spent no time now pondering Shemaiah's words. They were clear and needed no pondering. Judah threw his legs over the side of the bed and let his feet reach to the floor. He stood himself up, found yesterday's blue jeans, and dug a clean sweater from his drawer before hurrying to the bathroom. He had no idea who was waiting for him in the kitchen, but just in case, he thought it a good idea to stop and take a peek in the mirror.

The boy was glad he did. Oh, how he must have tossed and turned last night when he finally fell asleep. His hair was a crazed mess of wild. He did his best to fix it and half-heartedly brushed his teeth.

As Judah dried his hands and left the bathroom, he chuckled at how his hair could have possibly gotten so wild, and as he did, thought of Sam and his wild mess of red curls. As he thought of Sam, Judah's mind was quickly drawn back to Trilleah and more importantly, to Jennifer's story.

No wonder he had a headache. No wonder his hair had gotten completely unruly. No wonder he'd slept so late. Jennifer's story came flooding back and nearly pushed the curiosity of who was waiting for him in the kitchen right out of his mind.

He was thoroughly bewildered as he stepped into the kitchen, and it was apparent from the reactions of those waiting for him, that his face matched his mind. Bewildered ... flustered ... anxious ... curious.

"Judah!" came the angelic voice of Kaija Mae. "I thought you must have gone back to sleep." Jennifer laughed, and Judah was surprised by that laugh almost as much as he was surprised to see Kaija Mae standing in his kitchen.

"Kaija Mae," he sputtered. "How nice to see you. Surprising, but nice. What are you doing here?" As he heard the words that rattled off his tongue, he realized it might sound rude, and so before anyone else could notice, he added a second question to cover up the first one. "When did you arrive?"

He sat at the table and Bella handed him a large bowl of hot oatmeal smothered in honey and milk. "Thank you," he muttered, not taking his eyes off of the visitor. Judah had a feeling that the visit was not for anything good, and he waited anxiously for whatever information of the Dark Land that might project from her lips.

Kaija Mae pulled out a chair and sat down across from the boy. Jennifer was already sitting, eating her oatmeal, and now Bella handed Kaija Mae a mug of hot chocolate before grabbing her coffee and finally sitting down herself.

Judah wondered if he was the only one who knew nothing of the visitor's reasons for being here, or if maybe they all sat waiting for the answers to the same questions that were bouncing around in his mind.

He didn't need to wait long. Bella answered his question straightaway—by asking one of her own.

"OK, Kaija Mae. We're all here now so tell us the reason for your visit. Certainly, it's not just to have hot cocoa with us."

"No, you're right." She spoke quietly and sipped her cocoa. "I came here to you all because there is movement—a shaking really—in Trilleah, and I'm afraid you will need to make a Winter Solstice trip after all."

Kaija Mae didn't even act as though she'd just dropped a bombshell on her friends and took another long sip of cocoa without any expression whatsoever crossing her face. She looked around the table at the three faces staring blankly back at her. Both Judah and Bella had the same expression: dread, agitation, worry, hesitation. Jennifer had a different expression altogether.

Her hard stare had softened with the news, and Kaija Mae was surprised by her reaction. She had been nervous to bring the news to Jennifer in particular, fearful that she would refuse to return. The only way Kaija Mae even knew that Jennifer had survived and been returned to Westlock was because her Shailma had told her so.

Regardless, Kaija Mae was relieved by Jennifer's reaction and directed her next statement specifically to the young girl who showed incredible strength and perpetual peace. Suddenly, Kaija Mae wanted to understand where these things were coming from.

"Jennifer, doesn't this upset you? You don't seem surprised."

"Not really," Jennifer stated. "Simeon told me not so long ago that things in Trilleah had changed and we would be returning for the Winter Solstice. I've been waiting for you, Kaija Mae."

Bella's and Judah's feelings both bubbled over now.

"What?" Judah spouted.

"When did he say this?" Bella demanded to know.

"About four days ago, I suppose," Jennifer replied. She continued to eat her oatmeal as though the worst news ever had not just landed on their kitchen table.

"And you never thought to mention it to us?" Bella demanded again.

Now Jennifer was cross with her auntie. She set her spoon down and wiped her mouth. She looked directly at Bella and spoke with a firmness that none had ever heard come from her before.

"Um, yes Auntie, I did think to mention it to you," the annoyed girl said with much sarcasm and eye rolling. "However, as I was running to find you and Judah, Simeon stopped me."

"He spoke very clear to my ears—not to my mind, but to my ears—and told me that I was most definitely **not** to share this information with either of you for another would be coming to tell you both and it was not my information to share."

"They won't receive this news from you, Jennifer," he told me. "You must keep quiet and wait patiently, Jennifer. I will send someone from the Dark Land itself to deliver the news and make the truth known."

She looked to Kaija Mae now, whose eyes were large as she listened to the intense authority coming from this usually quiet girl.

"Now, here is the messenger from the Dark Land who Simeon promised to send." With that, Jennifer picked her spoon back up and continued with her oatmeal.

"Why are you not upset about this?" Judah asked. "I would think that out of anyone you'd be the one who'd refuse to return to Trilleah—ever!"

Bella said nothing, but her mind rushed back to the moment when she had heard Judah's heart-wrenching sobs as he watched the ground close over his sister. Bella wasn't sure she could handle any more situations with such painful outcomes. Perhaps it would be she who would refuse to return to Trilleah.

"Judah, as I told you last night, all things are as they must be." Suddenly, Judah's forgotten headache returned with a vengeance.

"Yes, but I still have no idea what that means so forgive me if I don't agree."

Chapter 7

To Be Willing

Judah slammed his mug down on the table. He rubbed his head and got up. He headed downstairs, yanking the door closed behind him. The boy was angry; not angry that his sister knew things he did not know or that she understood things far beyond his understanding. He was angry because he didn't want another trip to Trilleah. Especially when this old lady in a young woman's skin came to call them back to the horrible

Dark Land and say such statements as, "things are shaking in the land." What does *that* mean? Things are shaking … what does that *mean*?

He knew he shouldn't have slammed the door, and if this was not the situation it was, Bella would have most certainly opened it and started hollering down at him about ridiculous things like "Control your temper" or, "Get back here and shut this door properly, young man." But this was not a temper tantrum, nor was it just an ordinary angry outburst.

Oh, the frustration of such news was heavy. It felt like an anvil had been set on his shoulders and it was far too heavy to carry, yet there was no option of setting it down.

The girls remained in the kitchen and Bella did not get up to holler at the boy. She knew full well what he felt, for she felt it too. She was just too old and responsible to slam doors, but perhaps if Kaija Mae wasn't sitting at their table, Bella may have slammed something as well.

"He'll be back," Jennifer leaned in and whispered. "He needs time to process all this havoc and what-have-you," she added. The young girl was exactly right; she knew her brother well. Once Judah had some time to think and speak with his Shailma, he'd calm down and be back. That was just his way.

Down in the basement with the door shut, Judah began to rant. "Shemaiah, what's going on?" he asked out loud, hoping for an out loud answer but not expecting one. "Why did Jennifer know this news and I am only finding it out now? And WHAT does it mean, 'all things are as they must be?'"

"Shemaiah, I need answers!" He wasn't exactly shouting at his Shailma, but he wished he could have been brave enough to do so. Judah had waited only a moment before he heard the calming response from Shemaiah. He was disappointed the answers were only in his mind and not out in the air where he'd have preferred them. Nonetheless, he listened carefully.

My dear boy ... Judah, quiet yourself now and listen. I won't repeat my words. Judah did what he was told and quieted his heart. He put all other things out of his mind as best he could, and listened.

King Shrailzhar is trying to destroy his land. Judah went to speak, but Shemaiah hushed him. *Now is not the time for questioning my words, dear boy; listen and listen carefully.*

Judah hushed.

The king is making plans to destroy his land so the Curse Breakers cannot find their way back—so there is no land to return to. He would rather destroy his own kingdom, taking the cursed souls already trapped there into the abyss of Acheron and steal no more souls, than to lose the souls of the ones he already has. King Shrailzhar is willing to lose his entire kingdom if it means keeping the cursed souls as his own.

Judah, what you do not realize, nor understand, nor even have the ability to understand, is how profoundly wicked King Shrailzhar is. There has never been one like him before, and there will never be one like him again. He has been given reign over Trilleah, but he's willing to give up that reign because he knows his end is coming soon.

However, he will not be put to death, as many believe. He will be confined to another place—but a place where he has no power whatsoever, for it will be removed from him. His only hope—and may I say his entire purpose—is to steal and take as many souls with him to this new place called Acheron, to where he will be confined for all eternity.

That pathetic and weak king knows his time in Trilleah is short since nearly all the clay tablets have been found. There is one, though, who has no fear, whose trust in her Shailma is so intimately deep, that she will give her life if that's the price to be paid for freeing the cursed souls.

A lump formed itself in Judah's throat; he knew who Shemaiah was speaking about. He didn't want to admit it to himself nor have Shemaiah tell him, for once he knew, he could not un-know. Nevertheless, Shemaiah continued whispering the one thing to which Judah desperately tried to close his ears.

Judah, that one is Jennifer.

"NO!" Judah wailed, but even as he heard the word come from his mouth, he knew in his heart that was exactly the way it was supposed to be and there was nothing he could do to change it. Shemaiah waited a couple of minutes, giving Judah time to process this idea, and then cautiously continued.

The Shailma did not wish to overload the boy with too much weighty information, yet there was a great need for Judah to have as much information as he could handle before returning to Trilleah. Finally, Shemaiah continued.

Shrailzhar has learned this truth, for he was sure Jennifer would give up in the adder's pit. He was confident that he could bully her and put so much fear inside of her that she'd never return to his land. When she retrieved the clay tablet from the fiery dragon's nest, however, the king knew he was wrong. He knew that if he couldn't defeat her, Jennifer would instead defeat him.

Judah, the king is afraid of Jennifer, although he will never allow any of the Travelers to know this, and he will do everything— EVERYTHING—in his power to end her before she can end him.

The king has begun the destruction of his land. If you cannot get the remaining clay tablets before that happens, every soul that he has cursed and locked in Malleana Forest—and every soul that his miserable Trows are out stealing even this minute—will be lost in the abyss of Acheron for all eternity; your mamma included.

Time will come to an end, Judah. Time in Trilleah has nearly run out. The souls can be saved, but only if you move quickly, work hard, become fearlessly fierce, and believe that all things are as they must be. Whatever comes your way in Trilleah, believe there is something greater in charge of it, and no matter what happens, it is the way it must be for a purpose much larger than you know—for reasons far greater than you can see or comprehend or understand or imagine.

Are you willing, Judah?

Judah said nothing because he was in shock of such unutterable things that his Shailma had dared to reveal. Jennifer had said nothing about this nest of a fiery dragon Shemaiah had just mentioned, and Judah was somehow stuck on this one point. It was clear that even still, after all this time, his sister had left important details out of her telling of the adder's pit, and he wondered frantically if he could ever go back or better yet, if he could keep his sister from returning.

He pondered and wondered and contemplated these things deep in his heart, and when he was finished doing that, he considered them a little bit more. Oh, how he wrestled with such things. Finally, all the wrestling was interrupted by his Shailma.

Judah, Shemaiah asked a second time. *Are you willing?*

"I am," he answered calmly. He didn't know where the calmness came from, but as he heard it swaddling his answer, he felt it fill him up and suddenly, he understood Jennifer's statement. Nobody had explained it to him, but he understood. Judah repeated it out loud with a new boldness, a new fierceness, a new understanding.

"Indeed, all things *are* as they must be," he said firmly as he reached the top of the stairs. Quietly, Judah turned the knob on the door, pushed it open, and stepped into the kitchen. He found the girls still sitting at the table. None of them were saying anything but were quietly sipping their hot cocoa, which was no longer hot, for he had been battling with his Shailma in the basement for quite some time.

"Judah," Kaija Mae called. She was very calm, as though she knew what had occurred in the long minutes he'd been in the basement. "Are you willing?" she asked. Judah didn't even pause to wonder how the girl knew to ask the same question Shemaiah had just asked of him.

"Yes," he answered and sat back down at the table. "I am."

"OK then," she said. "Let me tell you what's happening—or give you as much information as you require for now. Very soon you will be returned to Trilleah and believe me, things in the Dark Land are not how you remember them to be."

"What do you mean?" Bella asked. "Willing for what?" And then, much to Judah's delight—and horror—he heard Kaija Mae describe to Bella and Jennifer what Shemaiah had just told him.

"The king is destroying his own land," she said.

Bella shrieked but Jennifer didn't react; neither did Judah. Bella seemed to be the only one who didn't know such things. It was clear to Judah that Simeon had given his sister the same information that he had been informed of now. But Bella's reaction—and sharp focus on what Kaija Mae was saying about Trilleah and King Shrailzhar and the cursed souls—indicated that she knew nothing of what was happening.

How is it, Judah thought, *that Bella knows nothing of this? How is it that Jennifer's Shailma told her, and my Shailma told me, but Bella—who at one time was the first to know anything—was now the last to know? And this, of all information, seems incredibly important information to know for the one in charge!*

Judah was only thinking these thoughts silently, but Shemaiah apparently thought he needed a response.

Bella is not in charge, Judah. Bella has never been in charge, although it may have appeared to be that way from the beginning of your journeys.

Judah sat listening to his Shailma as well as to the information Kaija Mae was giving, just to be sure he didn't miss anything. And apparently, he hadn't, for Kaija Mae gave no more information to Bella than Shemaiah had given to him. He did wonder, however, if perhaps Jennifer knew more than the both of them and by all means, she did.

This was not the time to share such information, though, and Jennifer kept quiet, sipping on the last few drops of her cocoa, now cold and thick.

Judah noticed as his sister repeatedly nodded in agreement to the information Kaija Mae was laying before the three of them. He also noticed the color come back into her face. She'd been pale since her return from the adder's pit. Now, her cheeks were rosy and her lips had returned to their bright pink color. He noticed the corner of her lips turn from the downward position they'd been in for months; nearly—but not quite—into a smile.

He found all of his noticing very odd and somewhat disturbing. Jennifer saw Judah watching her and gave him a quick wink, which he found even more disturbing. How could she be finding this information, of all things, good? Shouldn't she have thought such an unexpected return to Trilleah downright unacceptable, unreasonable, and altogether deplorable?

He planned on speaking with his sister about it at the very first opportunity he had. He would not have to, however, for as he continued to listen to the conversation being laid out in front of him, the answers to all his questions came.

"Now Jennifer," he heard Kaija Mae say. "Are you strong enough to return? I know the last trip was unbearably tragic for you and it must have done you much damage."

"I'm feeling strength return even as you speak," was the answer from Jennifer's lips. "To be honest with you, Kaija Mae, the last trip was horrible, but as Simeon has been explaining and helping me understand, all things are as they must be. So," she paused and rolled the end of her hair between her fingers—like she used to do with her father's curly hair when she was upset—"it must be so that I should return. That is why I am OK with it."

"I know that Simeon will be with me. The time in the adder's pit—having the serpent himself stare me straight in the eye and see right into my soul," Jennifer shuttered at the thought, "taught me many things."

"What kind of things?" Kaija Mae questioned.

"That I am always safe with Simeon," Jennifer answered straightaway. "I understand that it was necessary for me to be in that horrible pit—even though it seemed like the pit of hell. It made me want to fight all the harder and collect all the tablets even more because if that was not hell, and the souls of the lost ones will be banished to hell for all eternity unless we break the curse, then hell must be so horrific that my mind cannot even conceive it! I don't even dare to try!

"Indeed," Jennifer continued. "I will return and whatever comes is what must be. I will trust Simeon because I believe that if I did not have what is needed to do whatever is required, then I would not be there in the first place."

Now, Jennifer looked right into Judah's eyes and touched his hand. She felt he was becoming saddened by her words.

"My Shailma will protect me, whatever comes. Whatever comes, it must be part of what is needed to break the curse. I trust him,

Judah," she said as she continued to look through his eyes and into his soul. "I trust Simeon."

The boy rubbed the corners of his eyes and tried to force a smile, but he couldn't force much more than a slight turn of the corners of his lips.

"It's settled then," Kaija Mae spoke up. "The Shailmas will come to retrieve you in three days and you will return to Trilleah." Now it was her turn to touch their hands. Kaija Mae laid one of her hands over Judah's big hand and the other over Jennifer's small, fragile one.

"All things will be as they must, and more power to the Shailmas to get you safely through." And with that, Kaija Mae was gone, riding on the wings of her own Shailma straight back to the land of Trilleah, where the shaking had only just begun.

Chapter 8

3 Days

Bella and the twins sat without any words or movements, surprised that Kaija Mae had come—but somehow not surprised to see her go.

"One thing which Kaija Mae did not mention," Jennifer said, "was that, of course, she, Aviel, and the others who were wrongly taken to Trilleah would also be lost for all eternity. If Shrailzhar can destroy his land before the curse is broken, they too will be lost in an abyss of Acheron … forever."

"I never even thought of that," Judah remarked.

"The horrible truth that Kaija Mae seems not to realize," Jennifer whispered as though the girl was still there and might overhear, "is that she is, in fact, under a curse—although a different one than those whose souls are in Malleana. Yes, she's under a curse alright!"

"I never thought of that either," Judah said again. He continued to be both amazed and annoyed at how little he knew while Jennifer, so frail and timid, always seemed to know more than him long before he ever knew much of anything at all. Judah got lost in his thoughts of such things and wondered about them.

Jennifer was braver than him, that much was clear. But how? Where did her bravery come from? She had not been brave or courageous at all—even just a year ago. When he was starting to become stirred up and annoyed by all these wonderings, his sister interrupted him.

"So we *must* go then ... without delay," Jennifer said calmly. This new calmness Jennifer had found was beginning to carry Judah to the very limits of his patience. He asked her about it, although he succeeded nicely in covering his feelings.

"Why do you seem calm about such a journey?" he asked. "In fact, you seem almost excited."

"Yes!" Bella added curiously. "I hear that in your voice as well, J. Please explain it because even though I feel a lot of things right now, none of them are excited or glad or relieved or anything positive whatsoever."

"Well," Jennifer began. "It's not excitement. Or, maybe it is." She seemed confused but settled, nonetheless.

Maybe this is what happens when one snaps completely, Bella thought to herself, *because it would appear this one has finally gone mad.* Bella continued to think thoughts such as these ones and ended up nearly missing Jennifer's few words of explanation.

"I know the things that must come to be in order to free the souls and release Mamma from the curse of the Trows. I'm not happy, but I'm no longer unhappy." Jennifer rambled on while the other two listened. "Content in what must be, maybe.

"Simeon has explained many things to my heart, and I know that I will be powerful when I sit on his back. When I'm in danger, he will spread out his wings over me and I will be safe beneath them. I am horribly afraid, but when I find Simeon, he calms my heart and covers that fear with something else altogether. The time is short; there isn't much of it left to break the curse."

As she put forth her best effort to explain all those things she knew in her heart, Jennifer waved her hands around wildly trying to demonstrate all she was speaking of, and nearly knocked her mug to the floor. Judah caught it and without saying a word, set it back on the table … nowhere near his flailing sister.

"Oops," she said.

"The biggest part of why I've been so quiet since the last trip was not because of what happened there, although," she paused and scratched her head, wondering. "That would make sense. It was a horribly dreadful experience, and I hope that is the worst of Trilleah. However, I fear it is not. Simeon was in that adder's pit as well, though, and he rescued me from it."

As usual, Jennifer had gone off on a rabbit trail, and Bella brought her back to their question.

"Jennifer, if that was not the reason for your being so quiet and sullen these few months, then what was?"

"Oh right," Jennifer said, shaking her head. Sometimes she was amazed that anyone could follow her chattering at all. "The reason is that Simeon has been speaking to me a great deal with very heavy information and instruction that I did not wish to hear. I've been writing most of it down, and when Kaija Mae came this morning, I knew that I'd heard Simeon correctly."

"Maybe that's why I'm calm," she pondered.

"I have known this particular thing—about the king destroying his land—for such a long time now, but had nobody to share it with. That could be one of the reasons I feel happier now. It's not happy really; it's more relief, I think."

"Relief?" both Bella and Judah asked together.

"Yes, relief. Relief that I don't have to keep such dreadful secrets and relief that we get to return for Winter Solstice. I felt like I had to find a way back before the land was destroyed, but didn't know how, since I don't know the way."

"But then Simeon said to me, 'I am the way,' and so I knew that if he came for me, Trilleah must be in grave danger and if he did not come for me, the Dark Land would be OK until we returned for Summer Solstice." As she rattled on and on, Jennifer could see in the eyes of the two listening that she wasn't making a bunch of sense to them. However, she'd never been good at making sense when it came to Trilleah. The things she knew on the inside somehow never came out right.

"Three days," Judah said.

"Well, I suppose I'll have to postpone our trip," Bella sighed. She didn't sound pleased about that and turned her lips down, pretending to pout furiously. The twins just shrugged their shoulders, since neither knew how much time and effort their auntie had put into planning the little vacation. It would have been stupendous. But now, all that fun would have to wait for another time.

Suddenly, one statement from Jennifer's many statements climbed to the top of Bella's mind, and she asked about it. "J, you said you had no one to share the information with. Why didn't you share it with me?"

"Or me?" Judah added.

"Simeon made sure that I knew it was not to be shared. None of it!" Jennifer sighed. "He said that the time would come when you would both know the same secrets, but that one would come from Trilleah to tell you and indeed, one did. He said you wouldn't receive it from me because you were not yet ready for such information, or to have it come from me."

"Well, we know it now," Bella said.

"And I guess we'll be going soon as well!" Judah added.

Jennifer said nothing more but got up and put her cup in the sink. She turned the tap on and let the hot water run it over. Her eyes watched as clear water ran into her cup, pushing out the dark, muddied bits from the bottom. She was somehow mesmerized by it so much that she didn't notice Bella telling her to turn the tap off.

When she heard Simeon's voice in her mind, she knew why her eyes were caught by the water. *Jennifer, this is a picture of what you will be doing in Trilleah. It is dark there—like the bottom of your mug. It is dingy and dark and murky, but you, my Little One, you are like the pure, clean water being poured in.*

That darkness is allowed to remain as long as you stay away, but when you enter Trilleah, it shakes because it knows you are the clean water that will stir it up. You are the one that will make all the darkness leave, and you are the Curse Breaker that will, in fact, break the final curse and release the caught souls into Heaven.

Trilleah is afraid of you, Little One; King Shrailzhar is afraid of you. All the creatures and beings in Trilleah are afraid of you because they know they can no longer hide. They know your eyes have been opened to them and that their time is soon coming to an end.

Jennifer stood, her eyes still focused on the water in the mug even though Bella had shut the tap off. Bella noticed her young niece had gone somewhere else in her mind—wherever that might be.

As Jennifer continued to listen carefully, Simeon gave a strict warning.

Jenny, even though it is YOU who will break the curse and YOU who will release the prisoners, you must be so careful never to take credit for such things. It is not you, particularly, who will do any of it, for you have no power of your own, but it is the power of the Shailmas through you which will accomplish all that must be accomplished.

Choose your words wisely and always give credit to the one whom it is due; never take for yourself what someone else gave you the power to do.

She thought about this deeply, for it seemed an odd warning to hear. She never asked to be a Curse Breaker. She never sought for such things, and in fact, if she knew at the beginning what the ending might mean for her, she would likely never have gone to Trilleah in the first place. But then, even as she thought such thoughts, she knew—deep in her belly she knew—that such decisions were never really up to her.

Simeon interrupted her thoughts. *Now, Little One, you must get ready for this journey. It will take from you all that you have.*

How can I get ready, Simeon? she wondered, for honestly, she didn't have the slightest idea.

Dear girl, you must eat good food for the next three days. Do not skip your breakfasts as you normally do; you will need a greater amount of strength and energy. Eat well. Do not stay up late and do not go to school, for you will need to store up your rest as well. I do not want you being lazy, nor watching television. You must spend these next three days with me. I have much that you will need for this journey. Seek me and listen ever so carefully!

"Well, that seems easy enough," she said out loud, even though she meant to keep the words in her mind.

"What seems easy enough?" Bella asked.

"Oh … um … nothing," Jennifer replied, embarrassed.

She darted down the hall toward her bedroom but then quickly came back to the kitchen. Jennifer threw her arms around her aunt Bella and squeezed hard.

"I love you, Bella," she said quietly and then before her auntie could see the mist coming into Jennifer's eyes, she turned and skipped back down the hallway, popped into her room, and closed the door.

"What an odd one she is!" Bella giggled to Judah. Inside, however, Bella was not giggling, nor chuckling, nor even smiling. She had a feeling that hug and those sweet words meant more than she knew. Both Bella and Judah knew that Jennifer had more information—more secrets—that she hadn't shared, and it concerned them greatly.

They also knew that three days would pass quickly and they were certainly not prepared for the journey they'd just been informed they would be taking. Judah and Bella must have been thinking the same thing, for at the same moment, they turned toward the other and sputtered the same two words.

"Three days!"

Chapter 9

The Scribbler

Jennifer untucked her scribbler from its hiding place under the mattress with one hand and grabbed her favorite pictures of Mamma and Daddy with the other. She moved to the spot in her room where she felt hidden and safe from the world—between her bed and the dresser —and slid down the wall until the floor came up and met her bum.

She carefully spread out the pictures and positioned them so she could see each one easily. Then, Jennifer opened her scribbler at the beginning and began reading. Page after page after page she read—not because she'd forgotten anything written between the covers, but because she wanted to see if she had missed some detail or note or bit of information. Some pages stirred emotions of regret, some sadness, some anger, some fear. No matter what page she read, it stirred an emotion and no matter which emotion it was, none of them were good.

Now she must somehow prepare to do it all again. From her experiences in the Dark Land, this journey would likely be harder than the last journey. In fact, Jennifer suspected that since the king was trying to destroy his land, even the land itself would be angry with Jennifer this time. It seemed like a reasonable assumption.

The land was never exactly inviting to the Travelers. However, it had often given some assistance here and there to the Travelers when it was most needed. On the last journey, the moon had wept large drops of blood for Jennifer, and the sun had veiled itself so that it would be blinded to what was about to happen.

The burning bushes were sometimes a help and once in a while the wind seemed to blow in a direction that was to the Travelers' advantage. Often the caves would enclose around them, hiding them from predators of the Dark Land.

This time, however, Jennifer feared that every corner of the land would be fiercely angry and rage against her and the others. She could not have been more right. Indeed, the land was beginning to shake, and it knew the Travelers were to blame for its upheaval.

She did not wish to return, and a thought—a most horrible thought—fell into her mind with a thud. *What if Trilleah is destroyed while the Travelers are still inside its gates?* As she pondered that thought, a second thought followed closely on the heels of the first.

Where did that thought come from because it most certainly was not the voice of Simeon and it was not a thought I came up with on my own, Jennifer wondered with trepidation.

Simeon heard both the thoughts; even the lies put into her mind by the evil ones could be heard by the Shailma. He answered Jennifer's wonderings straightaway. *The king has sent some of his Dark Deceivers to pack your head full of thoughts, Jenny,* Simeon said. *They are the Deceivers of Trilleah.*

Yes, that was the soothing voice she knew well. However, the soothing voice brought very unsettling words.

Dark Deceivers? she wondered.

The Dark Deceivers are entirely vile and repulsive. They are part of the king's army which are unseen. I won't open your eyes to see them for they do not need to be seen. There is no need for it. They have the ability to put their thoughts into your mind as a distraction, as if the thoughts were yours to begin with. They use their lying thoughts to plant fear and to distract and persuade. That, my dear Jenny, is where that thought came from—the Dark Deceivers.

Even though Jennifer had heard the whispers of Simeon, she had no words of her own to respond with. She was horrified at the information he was giving her and she wanted him to take his words back.

They want you to believe it is useless for you to return to their king's land because you will not get out and if you do not get out there is no use going in.

Jennifer, Simeon said, *do not listen to them. You mustn't dwell on any thoughts they plant into your mind. Rise against those thoughts the deceivers fill your mind with because you must win those battles that occur in your mind. It is of utmost importance that you do.*

But Simeon, Jennifer wondered and whined, *I don't know how to battle them. I do not have weapons to use against them nor do I have great or powerful things to say back. They will not listen to a little girl like me! That is simply a battle I cannot win.*

She picked up a picture of her and Mamma and stared into her mamma's big brown eyes as her heart listened to Simeon teach her the most efficient battle plan; the only plan that would work at all.

Oh, dear Jenny, that is not so, Simeon announced. *The Dark Deceivers fill your head with lies, and so, your weapon is truth. The Dark Deceivers cannot stand against the truth and they will flee far from it ... every time ... without exception.*

I can try, Simeon, she whined with a weak spirit.

Jenny, you must do more than try. You must succeed. You are not weak nor are you alone. I have given you the tools you require and the strength you need to win every battle that comes your way. Jennifer, you must stand firm and fight this battle that you cannot see. If you do not, then the battle that is coming in Trilleah—the one that you can see —will overpower you, and you shall not be successful against it.

The small girl cowering in her hiding spot between the bed and the dresser wanted to shrink down and hide. She wanted to climb under her covers and never come out. She wanted to disappear from all that she could see, and all that she could not see.

However, more than all of these things that she wanted to do, was the one thing she needed to do. That one necessary thing was to free the souls of Mamma and the others. And so, she did none of the things she wanted to do but instead, closed her scribbler and carefully returned it to the hiding spot under the mattress.

The small but brave girl took a gigantic breath and let it slowly escape from between her lips. She stood up and carefully set all the pictures of her mamma and daddy back in their place, arranging them carefully. And then, much to her surprise, Jennifer opened her mouth and words came out that even she did not know from where they came. She assumed Simeon spoke them through her—she assumed right.

"Now listen here, you Dark Deceivers," she ranted loudly. "You are nothing more than liars from that adder's pit of King Shrailzhar. You will not frighten me out of this journey and the land will not be destroyed while we are in it.

"In fact, the land will not be destroyed until every clay tablet has been found, the curse has been broken, and the souls have been released. Now, flee from me you filthy, lying rodents!

"GO NOW!"

When Jennifer had finished speaking the words she did not even realize were in her mouth, she fell to the bed exhausted. She listened carefully to hear something—either from the Dark Deceivers or Simeon—but heard nothing at all.

She waited for a moment and when mere silence hovered, she called out for Simeon. He answered straightaway.

They are gone, Jenny. You spoke the truth, and they could not stay and listen, so they fled straight back to the adder's pit from where they came.

They'll return, though, with more lies and more distractions. Beware, Little One. Be ready. Always be ready. Be on guard and ready for their filthy lies to attack your mind.

Jennifer wanted to ask more questions—many more. However, she was too tired and she let her brain be quiet. In only seconds, she was fast asleep.

Not long after, her door opened slightly and Bella stuck her nose in to see if Jennifer was OK. She had heard yelling coming from her niece's bedroom, and when she knocked and Jennifer did not answer, Bella became concerned.

"Oh dear," Bella sighed compassionately when she saw Jennifer was sleeping soundly. "She must be exhausted, the poor thing." Just as Bella was about to close the door, Judah stepped in behind her.

"Bella," he said, and startled her. She jumped.

"Ouch," Bella squealed as her elbow hit the door frame. Judah didn't notice and kept right on talking. Finally, Bella shushed him for fear he'd wake Jennifer, whom he hadn't noticed was sleeping.

Bella pointed to his room just across the hall and steered Judah inside. She closed his door softly and then turned to the confused boy.

"Sorry, Judah," she said. "I was afraid you might wake J, and she needs to get her sleep."

"Oh, ya," he muttered. "I didn't know she was sleeping. I was in my room and heard her shouting," he said.

"I heard her from the kitchen!" Bella replied.

"Do you know what she was going on about? Or who she was yelling at?" Judah asked. He seemed concerned but then again, he should be concerned, for all sorts of horrible things had happened to his sister since they'd begun journeying to Trilleah.

"I don't know anything about it other than I heard her shouting. When I got to her room, she was asleep," Bella said.

"Weird," he replied and rubbed his eyes with the backs of his hands. He, too, was tired but not about to admit it to his auntie. "Maybe she just had a bad dream," he said.

"Yes," Bella agreed. "That's probably all it was."

Jennifer would have been lucky if that was all it was, for the encounter she'd just had with the Dark Deceivers was only the beginning. Simeon never told her that those same ones could enter her dreams, but that was exactly where they ended up.

She could hear them, circling her and chanting horrible lies, but she could also see them—or something that she decided, even in her sleep, must be them. All around her, surrounding her like the Shailmas had surrounded her in the adder's pit, were dark unexplainable looking beings. They were hard to describe since they were too thick to be shadows but too thin to be anything else. They were too solid to be mists, yet somehow she could see through them.

Whatever they were, Jennifer knew they were the Dark Deceivers from the adder's pit, and she knew they had her surrounded.

One reached out and touched her ears and suddenly she could hear much murmuring. One reached out and touched her eyes, and she could see the words of the murmurings going up into the air, filling it.

The words that she both heard and saw were directed at her completely—like the words had formed daggers or swords of some sort. She began to shake. Jennifer saw the words *destruction* and *removed,* hover above her head. She heard *capture* and *destroy,* echo around her ears.

The words began weaving themselves together to form sentences and phrases like, "Lead her to the slaughter, " and "She shall be no more," and even "As one left in the desert without water," swirled and twisted all around her. She felt as though the phrases were death cloths from the olden days that she'd learned about in school recently—like when a dead person would be wrapped tightly with strips of cloth.

Jennifer tried to scream out, but as she opened her mouth, a strip of cloth was stretched tightly over it. She gasped for breath but found none. She felt her feet being bound and looked down to see strips of the cloth, which were fashioned from the phrases and words, wrap around them and up her legs all the way to her knees.

Jennifer felt in her dream as though she was being buried alive in these phrased death cloths. She tried with all her might to fight, to pull them off, but the more she seemed to wiggle and pull and yank and tear, the tighter they became around her. The very life was being squeezed from her, not by hands or chords or ties or anything other than words.

She looked up. Something was beginning to swirl above her, and the words the Dark Deceivers had been chanting and shouting were rising to form a giant cloud above her head. In a flash, two of the Dark Deceivers opened her mouth and held it open while a third grabbed handful after handful from this cloud of words and shoved it into her mouth, forcing her to swallow them all.

She felt sick and wanted to throw up but could do nothing about anything that was happening to her. When she had eaten the entire cloud of words, she heard one loud scream from all the Dark Deceivers who were now dancing around her gleefully.

"You will eat the words we speak to you, Jennifer, and you shall not know the truth, for we have shrouded the truth in lies … and in lies, you will surely die."

Jennifer let out one loud shriek and instantly woke up. She let out a second shriek as she tried to move her arms and realized they were indeed tightly bound. She couldn't move and she screamed as loud as her voice would rise.

Judah burst through her door, followed by Bella.

"Jennifer!" Bella wailed. "What is it?" But even as she asked the question, she could see that Jennifer had wiggled and jolted and twisted herself around so much as she slept that she'd managed to get herself quite caught up in her blankets.

Bella sighed in relief.

"Oh dear. You've cocooned yourself inside your blankets." As Bella began helping her niece get untangled, Judah saw the look on his sister's face and did not laugh. Not even a chuckle came from him for he knew—even without asking—that she'd seen something unspeakable and indeed, he was right.

Chapter 10

Waiting for Daylight

Later that evening as they prepared a late supper, Jennifer found a few minutes to share the dream with Bella and Judah, as well as some of what Simeon had told her about the Dark Deceivers and their tactic of lies. She never found it especially comforting to share much with them because Judah only wanted to protect her and Bella seemed to get jealous that Jennifer knew so much more than she did. Consequently, Jennifer was careful with what she said—and what she left unsaid.

They sat and picked at their supper, but none of them were very hungry, or very happy. There was surprisingly little conversation.

"Pass the milk," Judah mumbled.

"Don't forget to bring the clay tablet," Jennifer sighed.

"I won't," Bella replied.

Bella realized she was no longer the leader of the journeys and was having some difficulties accepting the fact that her young niece seemed to carry such importance in breaking the curse. She didn't understand, but Jennifer's role of utmost importance in the journeys was unmistakable.

Judah, on the other hand, was frustrated that he couldn't protect his sister; he'd always protected her. When they were younger and had begun middle school, some girls in the class were nasty to her. He would come to her side and the bullies would leave her alone. Or when they were little and Jennifer did something silly or broke something and got into trouble, Judah would often take the blame so she could avoid punishment.

Now, when she needed his protection the most, he had none to give. It saddened him deeply and caused him to feel useless, although Shemaiah had told him time and time again that Jennifer would need him throughout the journeys, but not necessarily in the ways he wanted to be needed.

As they finished their supper and began cleaning up, Bella came back to the idea of the Dark Deceivers' lies.

"Jennifer," she said. "How did you know what the truth was to use against the Dark Deceivers? I understand that truth would work to overcome lies, but if one doesn't know what the truth is, then I would wonder how it could be used as a weapon."

"I don't know," she responded and shrugged her shoulders. Sometimes she looked like such a little girl to her auntie; this was one of those times. She had a look of innocence on her face that made Bella want to tuck her away and never let her leave the house again. "I just opened my mouth and the words came out—really loudly!" Jennifer laughed as she added this last part and a few bits of the peas she was chewing on spewed out. This made the three of them laugh, and before long, they were having a typical fun evening of horseplay and foolish shenanigans.

They played a couple of board games and since the Shailmas had instructed them to stay home from school for the week and "prepare for your journey," the twins stayed up later than was usually allowed. What "prepare for your journey," meant, none of them knew exactly—other than the few basic instructions Simeon had given—and how they were supposed to prepare for something so out of their control was a mystery. Nonetheless, both Judah and Jennifer were more than happy to stay home from school, and Bella had no work for the rest of the week anyhow. It would be the twins' 14th birthday soon, but that seemed to get lost somewhere in all the commotion of this particular journey; the journey they thought would not come but was now coming quickly.

As the twins were watching some videos, Jennifer remembered that Simeon had instructed her to get as much sleep as she could. She jumped up from the rocker as if in a panic and said a quick "good night," before heading down the hallway to her room.

"She's getting more and more odd," Judah said.

"I couldn't agree with you more," Bella added. The two of them stayed up a while longer until finally, Judah gave in to his eyes that kept falling closed.

"I'm tired," he sighed. "Goodnight, Bella," Judah mumbled as he headed to his room.

"Good night, sweet boy," Bella said and patted him on the leg as he walked past her.

She sat in the chair a while longer, enjoying it's comfort, and was deeply satisfied with how the twins were growing up. "Oh, Molly, you would be so proud of them," she whispered. "Judah is looking more like you every day, Theo," she added as she freed the words into the air. Sometimes she felt as though she could sense Molly and Theo in the room with her and when she did, she would speak to them as though they were right there beside her.

This was one of those times, and so she remained in the chair for much longer than she'd planned, finding some comfort in her quiet conversations.

Finally, after dozing off and on in the chair for a good while, Bella stood herself up. "Good night, Theo. I Love you, Molly," she whispered into the air, and for just a second, she thought she felt a warm breeze blow past her.

Bella shivered and headed toward her room. *This will be a long three days*, she thought, even though only two days were remaining before the Shailmas would come for them.

And those two days would fly by much too quickly. They all slept in and stayed in their pajamas for most of the time. Nobody left the house, and even when they ran out of milk, they decided to get it later. After all, it was dreadfully cold outside, and staying indoors in warm pajamas drinking cocoa made with water rather than milk seemed perfectly acceptable!

Each seemed quieter than usual, however, and one thought it was because the others were spending much time with their Shailmas. They all would have been correct. This was precisely what "prepare for the journey," had meant. But even as they did so, they were unaware that this time had purposely been set aside by the Shailmas for the Travelers' preparation.

The night before Winter Solstice was a long one. It was by far the coldest night so far this winter—or of any winter, it seemed—and the house had a deep chill set in it. It seemed that no matter how many sweaters or pairs of socks the twins put on, they remained chilly.

They each agreed that it would be good to pass the evening by making popcorn and watching a movie and maybe even sleep on the couches in the living room. When Jennifer went to grab her tattered red blanket and a pillow from her room, she noticed something odd. The pictures on her dresser looked different somehow, but she couldn't seem to figure out why, exactly.

Jennifer wondered if they had been moved, but that didn't seem to be it.

"Judah," she hollered down the hallway.

"What?" came his manly voice from the living room.

"Come here," she shouted back.

"Why?" he asked.

"Because!" she answered.

Judah huffed, as though walking down the hall was much too big of an inconvenience.

"What?" he asked as he turned into the hallway and saw Jennifer standing in her doorway waiting for him.

"Were you in my room?" she asked.

"No, why would I be in your room?"

"I don't know, but the pictures of Mamma and Daddy look different," she replied. "I don't mind if you were, I just wanted to know why the pictures look different."

"Let me see," he said as he squeezed past his sister and headed toward her dresser. He picked up one picture and stared at it for a while before setting it down and picking up another. He repeated this time after time and finally, he set the last one down. "I don't see anything different."

"OK," she said, "but something is different in here. I feel it."

"I don't know, Jelly Bean. Sorry, but I don't feel nuthin out of the ordinary," Judah said. But then he thought for a moment and added, "hold on a minute, I'll be right back." He went out the door and within seconds, returned. He was holding something in his hand, but Jennifer couldn't see what it was.

Judah suspiciously closed the door, turned to Jennifer, and held out his hand. When she saw what he was holding, she gasped and held her breath for a moment. She could not believe he was holding that dreaded little green jar! But indeed, right in his hand, there it was.

"Judah!" she cried. "What have you done? Why have you brought that thing here to the house? That cursed jar!"

"Shh," he said and put his finger to his lips to hush his sister. "Lower your voice, Jennifer. If Bella finds out I have this, she'll kill me! I didn't mean to bring it home. Honestly, I didn't. It was an accident!"

"Yet, there it is in your hand!" Jennifer sounded fiercely angry, but it wasn't anger she felt, it was more of a fear. The last time she had held that jar, it had spoken many frightening things to her. She never wanted to see it again, yet here it was, right in her bedroom in Westlock.

"Jelly Bean," Judah tried to explain. "Remember when I told you that we had all gone to your Sleep Chamber in the hollow because we thought you were there?"

"Of course, I remember!" she huffed.

"Well, I didn't tell you that there was, in fact, *someone* there. Someone who shouldn't have been there. Someone who had this little green jar in their hand ..."

"Who?" she demanded to know and was annoyed that she was only finding this out now—on the night before their return to the Dark Land.

"Jennifer, it ... it was ... it was Miriam."

"WHAT?" she shrieked. "Why was SHE in MY Sleeping Chamber and why did she have this in her hand? What could she possibly have known about it? Did she go into my Chamber looking for it?" Question after question rolled off Jennifer's tongue, and finally, Judah interrupted her.

"I don't know the answers to any of your questions because her Shailma came and took her before I could find anything out. I asked her, but she refused to answer."

"She doesn't have a Shailma, or I don't think she does," Jennifer ranted. Her face was turning red, and she was outraged. Judah hoped it was Miriam she was angry with and not him.

"What makes you say that? Why would she not have a Shailma?" he asked. This conversation was cut short because as Jennifer opened her mouth to speak of the Mindbender, her tongue swelled up and she was unable to say anything more.

Judah just stood there … waiting … holding the jar and looking blankly at his sister. He didn't understand why she had stopped talking, so kept pressing her for an answer. Jennifer finally stuck her tongue out so he could see that it was not only very badly swollen but had been covered in little black spots which looked painful and indeed, they were.

It had been a while since any talk of Miriam had come up, and because the Travelers were not supposed to be going to Trilleah for an entire year, Jennifer had decided to put Miriam … and her Mind Bending … and the curses she'd put on Jennifer's tongue … out of her mind—until now.

Without thinking, Jennifer had tried to reveal secrets about the Reptilian Mindbender and now she had to suffer the consequences of it. How long her tongue would be painfully swollen was unpredictable. It had never been this bad before.

Judah felt horrible for his sister but was a little relieved that the conversation about Miriam and the little green jar was postponed. He stuck the jar in his pocket, reminding himself to make double sure he had it with him at all times until Shemaiah came to retrieve him. Judah didn't want to have to leave the little green jar behind—it belonged in Trilleah. Something told him that nothing from Trilleah should ever be brought to Westlock.

All the while the twins had been arguing, Bella had been hollering that the popcorn was ready, and where were they, and why were they taking so long. Finally, Judah hollered back.

"We're coming, Auntie." He looked at his sister and trying to make her feel less pained, said, "She has the patience of a mouse in front of a baited trap."

Jennifer wanted to laugh—really she did. Her brother's comment made no sense at all, making it that much funnier. But laughing was painful for the moment, so she only smiled a little and headed toward the kitchen. She would be having no popcorn for the time being and hoped Bella wouldn't ask why.

As the twins entered the kitchen, both of them noticed that Bella had retrieved the clay tablet from its hiding spot on top of the highest cupboard. They were glad she'd remembered but sad it reminded them that their Shailmas would be coming soon to take them back to Trilleah. None of them wanted to journey to the Dark Land, but it was necessary, and they were willing.

Soon they were all tucked in blankets with bowls of popcorn and sweet tea and napkins. The movie had been started, and all seemed well. But what seems to be is not always what is, and with Jennifer, all was not as it seemed.

Judah and Bella didn't realize that Jennifer wasn't watching the movie, but was instead listening to Simeon. He was giving her plenty of last-minute instructions, some she didn't mind and others she minded a great deal.

Nevertheless, he would be coming for her shortly, and she needed to sleep. She was afraid to close her eyes, afraid to sleep, afraid of what might come through her dreams. So, even though she very much needed sleep, and even though the words of Simeon riddled through her mind, Jennifer fought to keep sleep from embracing her.

It eventually did find her, and Simeon worked hard to keep the Dark Deceivers from attacking Jennifer's sleeping mind. He called for three Shamar Shailmas, and between the four of them, they stood guard as she slept, battling the ways of the Dark Deceivers.

They'd come in full force to attack the girl's sleeping mind, since they believed if they could attack her with full force as she slept, they would be able to win the battle and keep her from returning to their king's land. They hoped that if they could keep her out of the land, the king may change his mind on destroying it.

They may have been right. However, the Shamar Shailmas did a splendid job of keeping the Dark Deceivers from succeeding in their plan, and when the first light of the morning appeared just a few hours later, Jennifer woke, fully rested.

No evil from the Dark Deceivers had entered her dreams, and she opened her eyes with no thoughts other than, *the time is up, Solstice has arrived; Simeon will come for me soon.* Of course, she was unaware he had been with her all night long, watching over her and standing guard for the peace of her mind.

Jennifer was relieved to feel that her tongue had returned to normal, and as she lay tucked under the thick blankets listening to Judah's hushed snoring, a calmness filled her.

She gripped her tattered red blanket. Just as she fell back into sleep, Jennifer whispered four little words.

"OK, Simeon. Let's go."

Chapter 11

Power of Words

The words had barely been uttered before Simeon came and scooped up the one who'd whispered them. Immediately Jennifer found herself on the strong back of her Shailma and they were headed to Trilleah.

She didn't know what she was feeling … so many things whirled together in her mind she supposed, that it was hard to separate one feeling from any other feeling. She smiled, though. Glancing down at her hand, she saw the tattered red blanket she'd fallen asleep with the night before.

It was still wrapped tightly around her one finger, and she left it that way for a time. Jennifer didn't want to drop the blanket; it was the only sure connection she still felt with her parents. If she lost the blanket, that might be the last straw.

So much time had passed since Molly and Theo's accident that sometimes Jennifer wondered if she'd even remember them at all if many more days passed.

"Of course, you would, sweetie," Bella said each time Jennifer told her auntie of the fear. She still had her doubts, though.

It didn't matter either way now, for when she had seen her mamma in the adder's pit, she recognized her immediately. Even though Mamma's soul was not there, her once beautiful eyes were hollow, and it was only a thin shadow of her body, the connection between them which Jennifer had worried may be lost, instantly sprang up.

So even though it was terribly miserable and unspeakably ghastly in that adder's pit, Jennifer was glad to have received the answer to her fearful question. Even in the most horrid place she could imagine, a small piece of light poked through … Mamma knew her and she knew Mamma. Bella had been right all along, and Jennifer had wasted much time worrying about nothing.

Simeon, she thought, holding tightly to the tattered red blanket, *Will I see Mamma again this time? Will I go back to the adder's pit? Is she still there? Oh, what has that dreadful king done with her?*

Little One, who can know such things? he replied.

You know, Simeon, she thought but wasn't surprised when he didn't tell her. After all, as she'd learned in the adder's pit, sometimes it was better not knowing things that would happen before they happened.

Jennifer wondered about this and that and a few other unimportant things as she rode silently with her Shailma, but he was of no help to her whatsoever. He would not respond to her silly questions, and again, she wasn't surprised.

Simeon was usually quiet on the journeys between Westlock and Trilleah. Jennifer assumed it was because he had to concentrate, but she didn't even pretend to know the real reasons. It didn't matter either —his reasons for being quiet, that is. It allowed her time to ponder without him scolding her or interrupting her or piling more information on her than she was looking for.

Jennifer had plenty of time to consider things on this journey, so that is precisely what she did. She wondered about the Dark Deceivers and what lies they may try to tell her. She made up a few but realized how silly she was acting; to try to think like a Dark One. How altogether ludicrous!

It can't be done, Simeon laughed. He too, was finding her amusing and told her so. She was embarrassed because—even after all this time—she had nearly forgotten that he heard all her wonderings and thoughts and ideas and conundrums.

But since Simeon was going to pay attention to her now, Jennifer decided to ask him about a few things to which she did want answers.

Simeon, how did the Dark Deceivers get into my dreams? Why did I see all of those things? Jennifer waited and hoped … and hoped and waited for an answer.

The Dark Deceivers want to keep you from their land. Usually, the most assured way to do this is to cause great and terrible fear; the kind of fear that makes one unable to move. That was the reason for them attacking your dreams.

How they entered your dreams is simple. It's easier for them to get into your mind when you're asleep than when you're awake. When you're awake, you can be prepared and fight back. When you are asleep, you're open to their attacks unless they are bound and forbidden from entering your dreams.

"Huh?" Jennifer asked loudly, for truly she had no idea what Simeon was talking about as was usually the case when he explained things. Sooner or later, Jennifer would end up more confused than she started.

I am going to tell you a secret that most do not know; if they did, there would be many less Dark Deceivers to bother them. Jennifer listened intently. It's always exciting to know something that nobody else knows, especially when it comes to such things as Dark Deceivers.

You see, Little One, Simeon continued, *you have much power over the Dark Deceivers. They don't want you to know this, but it's the truth. And again, truth is the one power against which they are defenseless. So the truth is, Jenny, that you can bind them up and demand they not bother you while you sleep—while you are defenseless*

—and they must do what you've said. They have no option but to remain in the space you allow them.

But how do I do that Simeon? I have no ropes to bind them with. I'm surely not strong enough to do that even if I did have a rope.

Oh, Little One, Simeon chuckled, *you are precious. You see, it is that very quality that makes you such a threat to the Dark Deceivers, to King Shrailzhar, and to the curse of the Trows. It is your simple thinking and naivety that makes you powerful beyond your understanding.*

You don't try and overpower any such things on your own, and you are very aware that you don't have the might, the strength, or the power to do so even if you were brave enough to try. You believe whatever I tell you and even when you are deathly afraid, you obey.

Every time you do, you gain more power—even though you're unaware of it as it grows within you.

OK, Simeon, that's all fine, I suppose, but you didn't answer my question. I don't know HOW to bind the Dark Deceivers. Tell me this one secret; please! Jennifer begged.

Yes, yes, I will tell you.

First, the Shailma said, *you tell me a couple of things. How did the Dark Deceivers cause you fear?*

Well, Jennifer said and paused to think just a minute. *By telling me lies, I suppose.*

Yes; and how did you defeat them? Again, she had to think back. Even though it was not long ago, her mind was so filled with other things that such details often got lost in the mess.

Um, I suppose I defeated them with the truth.

There is one thing that the lies and the truth have in common. Only one. What was it, Jenny?

Now Jennifer was completely confused and wasted not even a moment to tell him so.

Simeon, please, I don't have the patience for such games today. Just tell me.

Jenny, lies are made up of words and truth is made up of words. The key is in the words. When you bind up the Dark Deceivers so they cannot enter your dreams, you use the same thing—you use words.

The key—your power—is in the words you speak.

But Simeon, there must be more than just that. There has to be! That's far too simple. You said there is a secret that few know, and now you are telling me that secret is words? It cannot be that simple!

Oh, but my dear one, it IS that simple. Most want to make it more confusing, and by doing so, they lose the power in the simplicity of it all.

"Hmm," was all Jennifer could say because she didn't understand but would ponder these things deep in her belly and eventually, she believed, they would make sense to her ... somehow.

As she pondered, she heard something beside her. Thinking it was Bella, or Judah maybe, Jennifer looked over and expected to see something familiar. Instead what she saw was not familiar at all and in fact, it was terribly frightening. She dug her fingers deep into the back of Simeon.

There, right beside her, were the Dark Deceivers from Trilleah. They were on both sides of her—a bunch of them—and they were riding on the backs of something that looked a little like her Shailma yet significantly different. The Dark Deceivers looked like wisps of black smoke; not solid beings at all but yet, they had a form to them and ghastly faces.

What the Dark Deceivers were riding upon were like shadowy figures, and while they were the same shape as Simeon, they were not defined. They had no face, and it was nearly impossible to make out their bodies at all. They too were wispy—like copies or poor images of the Shamar Shailmas.

Jennifer could see large black wings, yet not nearly as enormous as Simeon's, and they looked more like spider webs than wings. She also had difficulty seeing where the beasts ended and the riders began. They each overlapped the other making them look as though they were one being rather than two. Maybe they were …

"Simeon," Jennifer whispered under her breath. "Go faster."

No, Jenny, he answered. *There is no need to go faster. These Dark Deceivers are only trying to intimidate you into turning back. They have no real power over you. They are made up completely of lies.*

They have made themselves appear gigantic and powerful. That is not true, however. In reality, they are small beings, struggling to keep up.

Watch, Little One.

Simeon turned and blew a big blast of breath through his nostrils and Jennifer watched in amazement as all the Dark Deceivers fell away. They tumbled through the air, and while they did eventually get back up beside Jennifer, they had lost all power of intimidation and fear.

She had great difficulty believing what she was seeing and hearing. Simeon had given her such great insight, and it was starting to make sense to her. Those Dark Deceivers looked so small to her eyes now that she stopped looking at them … she paid them no attention whatsoever.

If they were trying to fill her with so much fear that she'd turn back and stay out of Trilleah, they were failing miserably. Any fear she may have felt, vanished. The small girl riding on the back of the enormous Shailma laughed at the Dark Deceivers and when she did, they fell away completely, knowing their power was gone.

"Oh dear," she sighed. "That was weird."

Simeon, where are Bella and Judah? She suddenly felt alone. No answer came, but as Jennifer waited for some thought to come from her Shailma, she saw the gates up ahead. She didn't wish to enter alone since the last couple of Solstice days provided dangerous entries through the gates. It made no never mind because despite what she may have wanted, Jennifer was alone.

Now especially, since the king knew full well they would be coming and had sent his Dark Deceivers to keep the Travelers away, Jennifer felt nervous about what traps might be set to keep them out.

"Where is everyone?" she muttered loudly. Again, no answer was given.

The gates were close now and easy to see. As Jennifer kept her eyes locked on them, she didn't have to look hard or wait long to see things she did not want to see. There was no sign that any other Travelers had passed through the gates yet and this caused her concern. She had never been the first Traveler to arrive and she didn't want to be the first one to arrive now. Nevertheless, here she was.

Jennifer gripped her tattered red blanket tighter and squinted to see into the dimness. Surrounding the gates, both inside and out, were hundreds—thousands even—of the Dark Deceivers. The king had undoubtedly expected the Travelers and spared nothing in setting a wicked trap. As far as her eyes could see on either side of the gates, Dark Deceivers hovered.

Simeon! was all Jennifer could think, for in the short time it took to think that one word, her eyes grew large and her ears throbbed with the deafening sound of a massive pounding BOOM as she saw the Solstice gates themselves crack right down the middle. One entire side of the enormous rock wall fell away, causing a tremendous explosion-like sound. Jennifer covered her ears, gripping tightly to her blanket.

One gate fell against the other, and as the Dark Deceivers scattered to get out of the way, Jennifer was convinced that the Travelers were already too late.

The land had already begun its destruction.

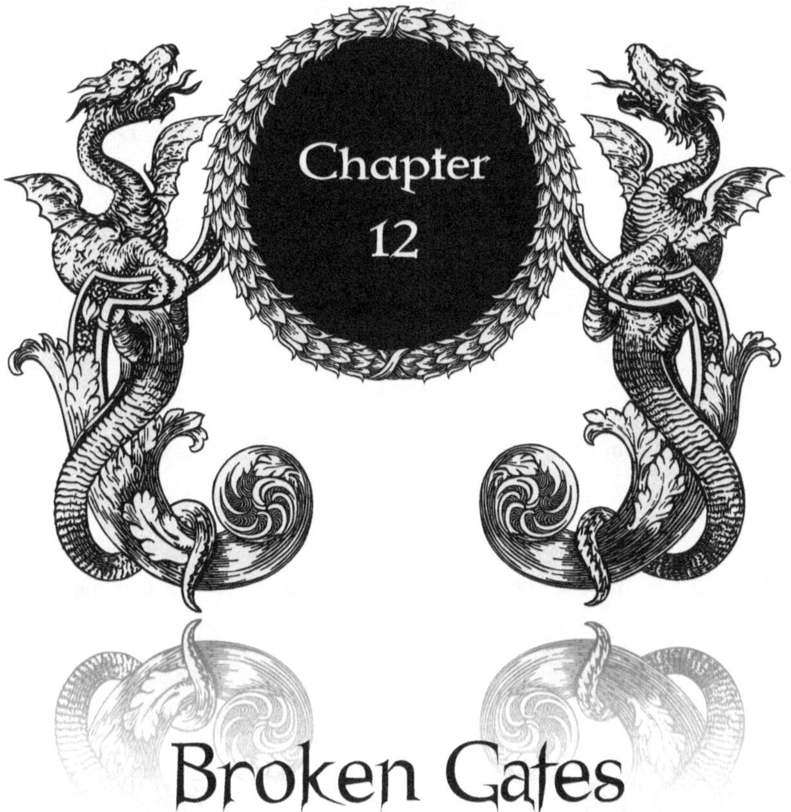

Broken Gates

Jennifer didn't know how he did it, but Simeon somehow weaved in and out and darted around, carrying her through the gates that continued to crumble. At least one side was crumbling; the other looked very unsteady.

A horrifying thought came to Jennifer's mind that chased her breath away. *What if no other Travelers can get through the gates?* Her breath remained gone, and even though she tried with all her might, she could not convince her lungs to fill up again. She took short, quick breaths, but the thought of being in this dark, crumbling land without anyone else was more than she could bear. Panic enveloped her.

"SIMEON," she cried out.

The ever-calm voice of the trusted Shailma came softly to her mind.

Do not think such things, Jennifer. Breathe deeply. I know you're afraid, but am I not with you? Am I not carrying you? Have you ever been abandoned by me?

Her breathing slowed, almost returning to normal as Simeon calmed her heart. She didn't need to answer; he was not asking the questions so that they would be answered. His questions were merely to remind her of what she already knew, and the fact was that Simeon *would* keep her safe—even if no other Traveler made it through the broken gates. She hated the thought, nevertheless.

Simeon took his rider straight to Asphelia's Hollow and set her at the entrance. He hadn't wanted her to see what was going on below them, so he had spoken to her about what was above until they had arrived at the hollow. Even though he had successfully distracted her, it didn't stop the chaos that was happening on the ground.

The army was panicking and running amuck. They'd fallen out of step and their chanting had changed. Their new chant was not something that Jennifer needed to hear since it was directed at her. Every being in Trilleah knew that King Shrailzhar was going to destroy the land because of the Curse Breakers and more specifically, because of Jennifer.

Every creature in Trilleah wanted to see the destruction of the girl before the destruction of the land. If the girl could be exterminated in time, the kingdom would be saved … unbothered for eternity.

There was nothing left in this land that would be helpful to Jennifer, but she was unaware of any of this at the moment, and Simeon would make sure she remained unaware of such things for as long as possible. The less she knew, the better.

As soon as her feet hit the ground, Jennifer thrust one foot into the small hole at the bottom of the rock and leaped into the hollow as it opened. She landed with a "thud" and even though it stung a little, she didn't care. At least she was inside!

Jennifer didn't jump right up; she was afraid nobody else would be inside, and she was in no hurry to know if that was the case. She did jump, however, when she heard a voice … a voice that was coming from very near to where she'd landed.

"Hello, Jennifer."

The voice was familiar, but not one she'd hoped to hear—ever—especially when she wasn't sure there was anyone else in the hollow; even more because she wasn't sure anyone else was returning to the hollow at all!

Now standing on her feet, she took a big breath and lifted her eyes to meet those of the unnerving girl standing directly in front of her.

"Miriam," she said flatly. Jennifer had no intention of being kind to the wicked Reptilian Mindbender but neither did she plan on provoking her. Jennifer knew quite well that Miriam had powers she could not battle.

"I've been waiting for you," Miriam sneered.

"Why?" Jennifer said mockingly, in the same tone of voice Miriam was using. If she was trying to intimidate the girl, Jennifer had grown far too strong for such games.

"I see your tongue has gone back to its normal size," Miriam mocked. "Honestly, Jennifer, do you not get tired of having it swell up like that? When will you learn to keep your mouth shut!"

Having these words come from the one who had put the curse on Jennifer's tongue enraged her.

"It was not swelled up whatsoever, so once again, you have no idea what you're talking about." Jennifer shuttered inside because it was evident that Miriam DID know what she was talking about, but how she knew was an unwelcome mystery. Jennifer was taking a risk just speaking to the Mindbender. She felt trapped, though, since there was no one around to interfere with whatever Miriam had planned. Jennifer begged for Simeon to come and throw the girl out of the hollow. Even though she couldn't see Simeon, she knew he was there.

"Don't think you can fool me, Jennifer. I am well aware that just last night you experienced a swollen and painful tongue." Then, just to taunt Jennifer a little more, Miriam added, "I hope it didn't ruin your evening." She laughed a horrendous laugh and Jennifer desperately wanted to know how this girl—clearly not one of the Travelers—had managed to snake her way into their hollow and the group of Travelers in the first place. Did no one else know what she was?

She dared not ask because it seemed that Miriam had powers that Jennifer knew nothing of.

"You know nothing of the sort," she huffed and pretended to head toward the passageway to her Sleeping Chamber. "Stay out of my Chamber, Miriam," she seethed on the way past.

Jennifer was rightfully frightened and had to pull her hands inside of her sleeves to keep Miriam from noticing how badly they were shaking. The last thing Jennifer wanted Miriam to know was that she was afraid of the Mindbender.

Miriam took a couple of steps toward the girl and blocked the entranceway to which Jennifer was moving.

"Move!" Jennifer demanded.

"No!" Miriam replied and let her disgusting forked-tongue slide out from between her lips. Her eyes went from the dark brown circles they normally were to an odd black line with a white dot in the center. The blood in Jennifer's veins turned to ice.

She didn't know what to do. The terrified and angry young girl didn't want to back down from the Mindbender, but she felt very alone and weak at this moment, with no idea where to turn. She moved to take a step around the horrible girl, but in that same moment, Miriam pulled her tongue back into her mouth and closed it quickly. Her eyes went back to their usual brown pupils and she stepped aside, moving toward the hollow's entrance. Jennifer, surprised at the change, turned to see that Bella and Judah had stepped inside the hollow.

"How long have you been here?" Jennifer asked, relief in her voice. She hoped it was long enough to have heard what went on with Miriam and to see how her face had become distorted. She was disappointed to find out it wasn't nearly long enough.

"We just stepped in," Bella said. "Jennifer, you left so early this morning; I was nervous to see you were already gone when I woke up." Judah tried to lighten the air because he could feel there had been something dangerous going on between Miriam and his sister.

"Yes, Jelly Bean," he said. "I wondered if you had left us behind for a reason ..." And then, just for Miriam's benefit, Judah added one more thing.

"I know your Shailma has been training you for any situation, and I've seen how strong and courageous you have become, so I knew you didn't need us here at all." He didn't laugh, or chuckle, or grin; even though he was talking to Jennifer, the words were intended for Miriam. He wanted the dark girl to know he was not joking and she needed to be very careful around Jennifer.

Neither Bella nor Judah said hello to Miriam, so she took the initiative.

"Well hi to you too," she said with much sarcasm. Judah responded with a nod of his head, but Bella ignored her altogether.

"Where is the basket of tablets?" she asked instead. Bella had pulled the one she'd brought from home out of her pocket and wanted to add it to the others, although the others were nowhere to be seen. "Miriam, where are the tablets?"

"I have no idea," she spewed. "How would I know? You sound like you're accusing me of something, Bella. Are you?"

"Not at all. It's just that you've been here longer than us, and you seemed to have a greater interest in the tablets than anyone else." Bella was being untruthful, but she knew that if she offended Miriam, the evil girl would not return the tablets. "I just wondered if you'd been looking at them again."

"How do you know I was here before Jennifer?" Miriam snarled. Apparently, Bella had made her angry already. "Maybe she took them for herself."

"I ... I," Bella sputtered. She knew Jennifer would not have taken them, but by saying so, Bella would have obviously been accusing Miriam. Instead, she said nothing and began searching for the basket of clay tablets.

Bella looked in every corner, nook, and cranny, but found no trace of the clay tablets or the basket that held them. She was convinced that Miriam was responsible for their disappearance, and was beginning to panic. *If the tablets are gone, we may as well go home and let Trilleah be destroyed,* she cried to her Shailma.

Shura responded immediately.

Oh, Bella, that's nonsense. Don't rush so easily into such harsh thoughts. Be patient and see what comes of this.

Bella wanted to argue with him, but she had learned long ago that arguing with a Shailma was useless and exhausting—a complete waste of time. So she did not argue; she decided to do what was instructed of her—to be patient and see what would come of it. Bella hoped that "what would come of it," was the basket of tablets.

Coming from one of the passageways the Travelers rarely used, Judah heard a commotion and went over to where Bella continued looking for the tablets.

"Bella," he whispered, "did you hear that?"

"Hear what?" she asked. She hadn't heard anything out of the ordinary and didn't bother to look in Judah's direction.

"Down that passageway," Judah whispered again and pointed toward where he'd heard the noises. "There's something down there. I heard it."

"Oh no!" Bella said louder than she should have since she alerted both Miriam and Jennifer to the problem.

"What?" Jennifer asked, suddenly panicked. As she looked toward where Bella was looking, there was a bit of a rumble, and the hollow shook. Some small stones and a bit of dirt loosened from above and fell, barely missing the Travelers.

"Oh no ..." Jennifer repeated Bella's words. "We can't stay here!" she squealed and began heading toward the hollow's entrance.

"We have to stay here, Jelly Bean, until the other Travelers arrive," Judah said. He went and stood by his sister in an attempt to keep her calm—and safe—in case more of the ceiling started to shake loose. There was no way they could leave the safety of the hollow just yet, even though it didn't seem to be all that safe now. It was Jennifer with whom the Dark Land was angry, so no matter where she was, the land would do its best to destroy her. Likely, that was what was happening now, but of course, they had no way of knowing such things and Judah dared not remind his sister of such a fact ... not yet.

From the passageway where Judah had been trying to get Bella to notice, there was another slight commotion, and automatically, Judah stepped in front of Jennifer. There was no need, however, as the ruckus that had been going on in the dim passageway suddenly popped out into the openness of the Eating Chamber.

Oh, how Judah laughed when he saw that all the while, it had been Pierce and Matt. When Bella looked over and noticed what Matt held in his hands, she ran over and threw her arms around him, hugging him tightly.

"MATT!" Jennifer squealed. She also headed to where Bella was repeatedly hugging the boys, and she joined in. So much hugging and laughing were going on, that nobody except Bella even noticed that Matt held the basket containing the clay tablets. He set it down quietly in the corner.

There was much rejoicing in the Eating Chamber as it seemed that many of the Travelers had safely made it through the crumbling gates.

"Has anyone seen Sam?" Judah asked. "Is he going to be stumbling out of one of these other passageways?" He chuckled, but it was more from awkwardness than anything else.

Nobody had seen Sam. But they did notice the looks that were exchanged between Pierce and Miriam. There was no doubt about it; something was going on between the two of them and when Bella noticed the looks, she was reminded of the first time she'd seen Miriam in their hollow.

She recalled how she'd overheard a conversation between them as they hid down that exact passageway from which Pierce and Matt had just emerged. As far as Bella could recall, those were the only two times that passageway had anybody in it. Now, she was curious and determined to find out straightaway what the connection was between the two of them.

"Pierce," she said, but before he could respond a clattering came at the hollow entrance and there, sprawled on the floor, were Sam and Aviel. "We were just wondering where you were," Judah announced.

"Well, here I am!" Sam responded. Jennifer skipped over and gave the boy who'd grown so very tall, a long hug. She sure did enjoy Sam—he was a funny one who always tried to answer her questions. Even on her very first journey, on the day of no questions, Sam had tried his best to whisper answers to whatever she may have wondered about; sometimes, even before she had time to wonder about it.

Now, his out of control hair was too high for her to reach, so the pieces of leaves that had fallen into the bright red curls would just have to stay there.

As the Travelers all chattered, excited to see one another again and curious as to how they all were able to return since they were all told *not* to return until the Summer Solstice, a loud BOOM interrupted. Silence flooded in and permeated the room. The only sound they could hear was the echoes of whatever had just made that piercing racket. It sounded like it was not too far removed from their hollow and for the second time in what would turn into a steady river of terror, fear moved in and gripped them.

Nobody dared say anything. Nobody tried to move. Everyone stood motionless (except for the trembling) and silent, waiting. Waiting for what exactly, none of them knew.

In the midst of them, though, right between where Jennifer and Sam were standing, Kaija Mae suddenly appeared. Out of nowhere, there she was. This was a curious thing, as the very odd girl seemed to appear and disappear quite regularly lately. Now was not the time to wonder about her travels, however, but instead to be exceedingly glad she was with them.

As the echoes quieted down and all that could be heard were some bits of rock and dirt dropping from the ceiling now and then, Bella spoke up. "Kaija Mae, I'm glad to see you. Where did you come from?"

"I wasn't far, just out in the Dark Land looking, seeing how much damage has already been done and where the worst of it is located. I must tell you, even though I'd rather not, that it seems the land is destroying itself from the outside in."

"Why would you rather not tell us that?" Jennifer asked. It seemed like a better thing to say than the land was destroying itself from the inside out. Every Traveler looked at Jennifer with puzzled expressions. "Seems like the hollow is safe for now."

How could she not know? one thought.

Surely she must be aware, questioned another silently.

Suddenly, the reason Kaija Mae's news was so terrible came to Jennifer's mind, but oh, how she wished it hadn't.

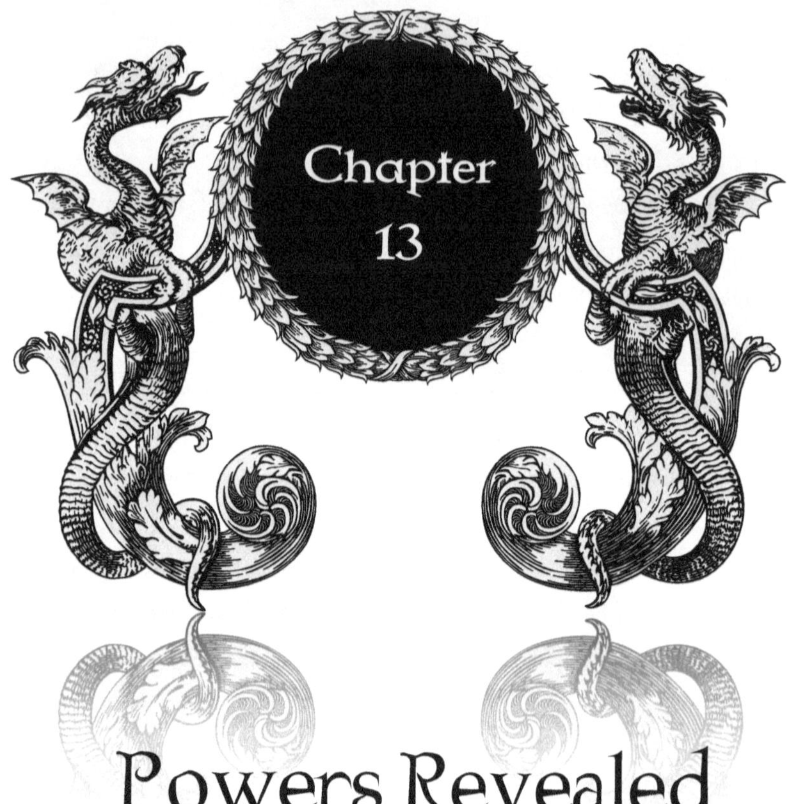

Chapter 13

Powers Revealed

A thought suddenly burst into her mind. *We are not the center of the land. The land is large, and we've never even traveled to the center—we probably will—but haven't yet.* All at once, Jennifer realized the gates were on the outside of the tragic Dark Land, Malleana Forest was just inside the gates, and Asphelia's Hollow was deep inside the forest. They were on the outside of the Dark Land; the very outside. As outside as they could get.

"Oh no!" she wailed. "What are we going to do?"

Bella patted her arm. "We are going to hurry and make some food to take—hopefully to the center of Trilleah. Pierce is going to gather the maps, and then we are going to get out of this hollow!"

It was clear that Bella had no idea what she was wishing for. The center of Trilleah was the most horrific of all places in this—or any other—land. If she had pondered the worst place imaginable, it would not compare with what lay in the center of Trilleah. If they ever had to travel there, if there ever came a moment when that is where they found themselves, she and the others would have begged for the land to fall in on them and destroy them completely. But she didn't have any idea, nor did anyone else, so their attention stayed where it was—on the falling stones and shaking dirt that was sprinkling down from above.

"That has to be why the stones are shaking loose," Pierce said. He hurried to the basket of maps and started digging through frantically, laying out one and then another, not waiting for any to burst to life. "I should take you all," he muttered to the ones still in his hand.

"Matt, you and Judah come with me to get food," Bella shouted. "Hurry!"

"Simeon," she whispered. "Help us." No words came from her Shailma at the moment, but something told her that he was near. Simeon was aware of the happenings and was helping, whether she had any awareness of it or not.

Jennifer noticed that Miriam had moved, unnoticed by anyone else, toward the basket holding the clay tablets. With everyone in the Eating Chamber, Jennifer felt empowered and raised her voice loudly.

"Auntie Bella, maybe you should take the basket of clay tablets with you," she suggested.

Miriam shot Jennifer a look that would have put the timid girl in her grave if she had been the only one there. However, because the others were also there, and because Miriam did not have her trapped in a secluded corner where she could whisper threats or let that wicked tongue lash out and sting her, Jennifer was confident enough to return the look. She glared with great boldness at the Mindbender.

Bella turned and saw what Jennifer had seen. Miriam was undeniably moving toward the tablets since there was no other reason for her to be heading in that direction.

"Yes, great idea," Bella said. She sent Matt over to retrieve the basket and bring it with him as she and Judah disappeared into the passageway leading to the kitchen.

Quickly, Matt reached out and grabbed the basket, but as he passed Miriam, she gripped his arm. It was only for a moment, but as she dug her fingers into his skin, a sharp burning pain shot through, all the way to his shoulder, and he dropped the basket. Two of the tablets tumbled out and broke in half.

"Miriam!" Matt scolded. "What have you done?"

Miriam had no reply, but Jennifer noticed her evil forked tongue fighting to get out and sting Matt, just as it had stung her in the Labyrinth. Instead, Miriam turned and ran into the passageway.

"What is with her?" Matt demanded to the others who'd seen the occurrence.

"Oh Matt, you'd be shocked if you knew!" No sooner had the words slipped from Jennifer's mouth than her tongue swelled up to double its size and large cuts began slicing their way into her mouth. They began bleeding horribly, and she was unable to speak.

Sam noticed immediately and ran toward her. "Jennifer, what happened?"

She could, of course, say nothing, but a thought came to her. She pointed furiously down the passageway into which Miriam had just stepped. She pointed to her tongue, wiped the blood that was now running from her mouth, and pointed again to the passageway.

"Miriam?" Sam asked.

Jennifer nodded her head frantically. Matt interrupted her game of charades by shouting and pointing.

"Look at this!" He had his sleeve rolled up by now to show where Miriam had grabbed his arm. It, too, had swollen up grotesquely and had three or four large gaping gashes. They had to wrap a rag around it before the bleeding would stop.

Jennifer was annoyed because the one time she had an opportunity to reveal some truth about Miriam, Matt had taken the attention away from her. Of course, what he really did was secure the story Jennifer was trying to tell without the use of any words, but Jennifer never thought about that.

Judah and Bella had heard the ruckus by now and had returned to the Eating Chamber to see what was going on. With the land shaking and hurrying to destroy itself, everyone wanted to stay close to everyone else.

"Jennifer," Judah urged. "Stick out your tongue." She did. "I remember last night as Jennifer tried to tell me something about

Miriam, that her tongue swelled up like this but instead of the cuts, it was covered in black bumps."

"Jennifer," Bella said, remembering other times when her niece's lips had blistered, or her tongue had swelled for no apparent reason. "Is this what happens when you try speaking of Miriam?"

FINALLY! Jennifer screamed in her mind since her tongue refused to work. She nodded frantically and her eyes began to water. She never considered that Miriam could do whatever damage she chose to do whether Jennifer spoke—or did not speak—of her secret.

She realized it now, however. Immediately her eyes began to haze over, and her vision became blurred. She began blinking hard, but the haze remained. She rubbed her eyes fiercely but the haze remained and thickened. The others noticed and ran to her side.

Sure enough, the whites of her eyes had turned to a dark yellow, and they looked as though a thick, sticky film had been stretched over them.

"OH, JENNIFER!" Bella shrieked. "OK, say no more, do no more."

Bella looked frantically around the room, which had begun shaking noticeably more by this time. What a complete disaster this was turning into and their journey had not yet begun!!

"Kaija Mae," Bella cried, "take Jennifer to the ..." but before she could get the entire request out, Kaija Mae interrupted her.

"I can't help Jennifer. I'm sorry. I must go after Miriam!" With that, Kaija Mae turned and ran into the dark passageway which hid the wretched Reptilian Mindbender.

"Hmph." Bella shook her head in overwhelmed frustration. "Sam, can *you* take Jennifer to her Chamber and help her splash cold water on her eyes? Anything you can think of to help, please do it immediately." Sam nodded and took Jennifer by the arm and led her carefully toward her Chamber.

Judah shouted after them. "Drink some water as well!"

"Now," Bella said, still fully panicked but turning her attention to Matt's arm. "What happened here?"

Matt began to tell the story, but as he did, his arm where Miriam had touched it turned a dark shade of purple, and the bleeding became much worse.

"Oh dear!" Bella shouted. "WHAT'S HAPPENING?" she shrieked, but of course, nobody knew, and that's who answered her question … nobody!

There was only one place left to go for answers—to the Shailmas.

"Shura," Bella cried out loud which was rare, but she was desperate. "What's going on?"

Judah joined Bella's plea for help. "Shemaiah, what is this power that Miriam has? Help us!"

Finally, Matt joined the cry. "Mishan, how can we stop her?"

There was much rumbling. Pierce was aware of it all but still believed he was doing the right thing by letting Bella deal with the situation as he continued digging frantically through the maps.

As every Traveler—except for Pierce—begged and pleaded with their Shailmas to help, to give them wisdom for such a disastrous situation, Kaija Mae was getting close to where Miriam had gone to disappear and find shelter.

"I know you're here, Miriam," Kaija Mae shouted down the passageway. It echoed all around, and she heard her voice come back to her. Following close on the echoes of her own callings, came the voice of the one for whom she was searching.

"Of course, I'm here! You can't stop me, you weak-willed, spineless weasel; my mind-bending powers and reptilian poison are given to me by the great King Shrailzhar himself!" Miriam shouted. "You have no rights to remove them from me."

"You may have power over the Travelers, but I am not one of them. I'm not a Traveler nor is my soul cursed, but you already know that."

"It doesn't matter; you have no power over me, Kaija Mae," Miriam wailed.

"You may have power over the Travelers," Kaija Mae shouted back. "You may have power to put curses on them to stop them from revealing your identity, but Miriam, you forget that you have no power over me!" She waited for a reply, but none came. "You forget that your power comes from keeping your identity a secret. If they know—if your identity is revealed—they will throw you into the sea!

"You overlook facts, you wretched Miriam. I can reveal your secret at any time, and when I do, your powers will be stripped from you, and it will be the end of you!" Kaija Mae was screaming now, and the echoes that were bouncing off the passageway walls were deafening.

Still, Miriam remained quiet, and Kaija Mae found this to be delightful for she knew that her point had been made. The truth had silenced the wicked Reptilian. One last point needed to be made, however, and she waited for the echoes to quiet themselves before making it. Finally, the opportunity came, and Kaija Mae took it swiftly.

"Miriam," she said loud enough that it was sure to be heard. "You will NOT curse any more of the Travelers, nor shall you cause Jennifer more pain. If you do, I will immediately reveal your secret." Kaija Mae raised her voice louder than ever before, to make sure the wretched Mindbender heard her and to make the words echo endlessly throughout the passageway so Miriam would hear her command over and over and over again. Kaija Mae knew about the power of repetition and used the echoes to her advantage.

"You are not to return to the Eating Chamber until the Travelers have left …" and just a bit louder still, "NOW BE GONE!"

No more words came from Miriam, but a cold wind blew through the passageway, stirring up the dirt from under her feet and the dust that was being shaken from above her head. Kaija Mae knew that Miriam had left the hollow and that she would not return while the Travelers were inside.

Calmly, she returned to the Eating Chamber to find everything had changed. Pierce had found the maps needed for the journey and had his cloak on. Jennifer had returned with Sam, and although her eyes were stinging fiercely, the yellow had faded and she could see clearly again; well, almost clearly.

Her tongue had stopped bleeding and she could speak. It remained swollen, so when she did speak, it made everyone chuckle since it sounded funny. Both she and Sam had their cloaks on as well.

Finally, Matt had re-wrapped his arm tightly, and the bleeding had stopped. It had returned to close its normal color but was still swollen. He was putting his cloak on as Kaija Mae re-entered the Chamber and she noticed that he had the basket of clay tablets. He would no longer let them out of his sight—even for a moment. Matt had been put in charge of keeping the tablets safe, and their discussions about where they may have disappeared to earlier revealed that Pierce had hidden them after the other Travelers had all left the hollow last time.

"I had a feeling," Pierce said, "they were no longer safe just sitting here in the open, so I hid them in a spot I'd seen in a chamber nobody else had been inside of. I knew they'd be safe there."

What Pierce did not know, was that Miriam had watched him hide the tablets and knew exactly where they were. He didn't know that Kaija Mae had to keep the tablets with her at all times while the Travelers had been away to keep Miriam from destroying them. What none of them knew, was that destroying the tablets was the sole purpose of Miriam being among them, her sole purpose in the powers she'd been given, and the sole purpose of her existence in the Dark Land.

She had not stolen them yet, even though she'd had the opportunity, because she knew that once she had destroyed the clay tablets, King Shrailzhar would have no more need for her. Even though she had a deal with the king, Miriam was wise enough to know that he was not to be trusted—deal or no deal.

CRASH went something on the outside of the hollow, and again bits of stone and handfuls of dirt sprayed to the floor.

"Oh dear," Bella sighed. She never voiced it for fear of causing more anguish to the others, but her thoughts were overrun with wondering if there would be a hollow in which to return. She didn't need to voice her wonderings, however, for every one of the Travelers' wonderings was the same as hers.

"Pierce, do you have the maps?" Bella asked.

"I do," he replied.

"Matt, do you have the clay tablets?" Bella wondered.

"You bet," Matt answered.

"OK, and I have the food." Just before they moved toward the entrance of the hollow, Kaija Mae pulled something from behind her back and held them toward the one who needed what she had.

"Sam," she said with a cheeky smile. "I thought you might want these." With all eyes on her, Kaija Mae handed him the Book of Truths and the Book of Lies.

"Where did you find these?" he squealed with much delight.

"I found them inside that passageway where Miriam was hiding," Kaija Mae said and gave him a mischievous wink. Sam held his hands out and took the books from her. He pulled them inside of his cloak, but instead of putting them in one of the many pockets, he held them tightly in his hands, afraid to let them go again.

"OK," Bella sighed. "Let's go," she bravely instructed, although she was trembling tremendously underneath her cloak. Great amounts of fear gripped her soul and no courage could be found.

Chapter 14

What Ifs & How Abouts

One by one, as each stepped out of the hollow and into the Dark Land, their mouths dropped open letting escape terrifying gasps mixed with dreadful sighs. In the short time they had been inside their hollow, Trilleah had changed.

Beneath them, there were enormous cracks in the ground. Above them, the sky looked as though it had been torn open here and

there. They could see large slivers of black peeking through the rips …
a black darkness like one had never seen before … a darkness that
threatened to break through and swallow everything in its path.

To make it all much worse, if such a thing could be so, sounds
echoed all around—painful sounds. The land was gasping as if it were
dying; perhaps it was. The sky was giving way to sounds of anguish
and cries, but the worst sound—the one that caused the Travelers' ears
to burn and their hearts to weep—were the ones coming from the forest
… straight from the souls of the Waiting Ones.

Oh, the pain of it all. Oh, the anguish and deepness of the
ferocious cries were more than they could bear.

"We're never going to make it," Judah wailed. "There's just no
way … I don't see any way through!"

"We WILL make it!" Jennifer demanded. "We've got to!"

"Maybe we'll find one tablet, maybe two, although," Judah
paused and Sam took the opportunity to finish his sentence.

"Although in all our journeys, we've never found more than
one, so it's unlikely we'll find two today … we'll be lucky to find one
without getting destroyed ourselves!"

Judah nodded at Sam as if to say, *thank you for finishing the
sentence I didn't have the courage to finish.* Sam nodded back as if he
understood the unsaid, "thank you."

"But we're so close," Jennifer argued. "We can't give up. We
mustn't!"

Again, Judah began a sentence which he could not finish. It
didn't need to be finished; everyone knew the ending without the

ending being spoken. "We need two more tablets," he said. "They are still out there somewhere. Even if we find one today, which is unlikely, the land won't ..."

They all knew the ending. Nobody needed to put words to it; nobody could. If it was unlikely that they would find any clay tablets this journey, it was even more unlikely that Trilleah would remain long enough for them to return one more time.

It seemed ridiculously pointless to keep going. If there was no chance of them finding BOTH the remaining tablets—which was what was needed to break the curse and free the souls of the Waiting Ones— why should they risk so much now to try to find either of the ones remaining? It made no sense.

"But our Shailmas brought us," Bella reminded everyone. "They must know it's not an impossible task otherwise they'd not have brought us— surely they would not put us at such grave risk for no purpose ..."

"I suppose," Judah said, sounding defeated.

All the while this pointless conversation of senseless trepidation was going on, the Travelers were wandering through Malleana Forest. They had no idea where they were going since the land had shifted and fallen so much. It was completely mixed up—like a puzzle in a box. Where the Carphlour Caves were once located, now stood pieces of the forest and enormous slabs of broken rock.

"Where are the Caves?" Pierce asked in shock. "How can we read the maps without the Caves to cover us? No, no, this cannot be ..." Pierce rubbed his head and looked around, getting more and more anxious with each passing moment. He kept whispering, "this cannot be happening … this just cannot be happening."

"Over there!" Matt suddenly hollered out and pointed to the spot where the Caves used to cover the Travelers and allow them to read the Living Maps. "They're still there, just behind all those boulders and bushes."

It seemed the land had rearranged itself to hide the very necessary Carphlour Caves and while it failed at hiding them, it succeeded in keeping the Travelers from entering.

"They are useless to us," Sam yowled.

All the while the ruckus and bellyaching had been going on, Jennifer talked to Simeon. Or, if the truth were told, it was Simeon who had been talking to Jennifer.

Little One, he said, *you are worrying greatly and trusting little. That is not the way. You must believe the Shailmas know things you don't for we see all, hear all, and know all things. There is time. There is still time to gather the remaining tablets if you stop wondering and worrying and carrying on. Doing so only wastes time.*

Listen to me; follow my leading and all will work out. All things are as they must be. Do not look around you, to the right, or to the left. Do not let your eyes wander up to the sky above or down to the ground below. Keep your eyes on me, Jenny. Keep focused on me; it is I who will get you through.

The land is filled with great deceivers and what you see is not what is. Do not trust your eyes for they will undoubtedly lead you down the wrong paths. No matter what it looks like, believe that it is how it must be and trust me to lead you. Can you do this, Jenny? Can you trust me to lead you?

The only thing Jennifer could think was, *if you lead me, I will follow you.* And although her words were few, she was firm in those few she did use, and Simeon knew it.

The Travelers stood not knowing what to do or which way to go, but Jennifer saw that just between the debris and enormous slabs of rock that had closed off the entrance to the caves, was a bit of space. She went closer to look and see what it was.

After only a couple of steps, everyone began whispering loudly, calling for her to come back. She didn't listen to them, though. It was not them she was following, it was Simeon. He was the one who showed her the space, and it was he who told her to go to it.

The others knew by now that when Jennifer had her mind set on something, there was very little they could do to change it. This was one of those times.

What Jennifer failed to see, however, was that King Shrailzhar was close. The others did notice this dreadful dilemma, though, which was their reason for calling her back so frantically. What the rest of the Travelers didn't understand was that while they only searched for their Shailmas when trouble came, Jennifer was always connected to her Shailma.

In trouble or peace, whether at school with her friends or home and alone in her room, Jennifer had found in Simeon what she could find nowhere else. Even Judah, who was closer to her than anyone else, could not give to Jennifer what Simeon could; peace. Simeon filled the deepest parts of Jennifer with a peace that was beyond any understanding; entirely incomprehensible or explainable or understandable.

Once Jennifer had experienced the peace which could only be found in her Shailma, a bond was made unlike any other. Even her beautiful mamma, or her strong daddy, could never fill Jennifer's insides with the peace she found in Simeon.

Jennifer often remembered that her mamma and daddy would try to change a bad situation or make the twins feel better when things were going poorly. When the coach of their soccer team wouldn't play the twins as much as they wanted to be played and Judah and Jennifer were annoyed or sad about it, Daddy would "have a chat," with the coach and try to change the situation.

Or one time when Jennifer's friends decided they would rather play on a Saturday afternoon without her and Mamma had found her crying under the bed, she went "outside for a walk." Jennifer knew that walk meant that Mamma would purposely run into her friends and try to change the situation so that her daughter didn't feel sad or rejected or whatever number of negative feeling she was carrying at the moment. That's just what mammas and daddies do.

Simeon was different.

He never changed the situation or gave Jennifer different circumstances. Instead, Simeon changed Jennifer. Over time, and in a perfect way, he earned her trust and she believed fully that no matter what happened, things would be as they needed to be … and that she'd be OK.

Simeon would make sure that even in her deepest hurts or sharpest anguish or most frightful fears, Jennifer would be OK because she trusted him. She had learned to trust Simeon, rather than what her eyes or ears or heart told her. She'd learned that often what she saw with her eyes was far from the truth. Simeon, though, always knew what the truth was. Now, in this Dark Land that was shaking and pulling itself apart, it was hard to trust her Shailma, but she was doing the best job of it that she could.

The others had noticed Shrailzhar coming and pulled their cloaks tightly around themselves, hunching down behind some boulders. Judah laid right down on his belly so he could keep an eye on his sister without being seen. Surely, if the king did his old trick where he threw dust into the air to see which way it would blow, he would find it useless today because the wind was blowing every which way. Today, it felt as though the wind was coming from the lungs of Trilleah, blowing hard one way, and then without any rhyme or reason, blowing hard the other way—almost like the air was being pulled in and then being pushed right back out again.

Judah wanted to shout to Jennifer and alert her to the king's presence, but he dared not. If the king didn't see her already, Judah did not want to draw his attention to her. What he couldn't see, of course, was that Simeon had already let her know and she was quite aware the king was behind her.

That's the reason she stood perfectly still with her cloak hood up, staying tucked inside the crack between the rocks. It reminded her of the space back in her bedroom—just between her bed and the dresser —where she felt safely hidden away.

Here, her cloak was the same color as the rocks, and it was especially dim out today. *If you are still, you will appear like a shadow to the king. But you must be still. Let him pass.*

Jennifer had seen the king before. She had looked straight through his hollow eyes and had him stare back into hers. She'd seen him grab her mamma and she had seen the Shailmas stand guard all around her. She knew that Simeon had protected her then; she knew he'd do the same now. Her belly still rolled, though, and she felt as though she might throw up.

I'm afraid, Simeon, she thought. *What if he sees me? What if the dirt balls he throws up, find me?* The *what ifs* went on and on and on and on, but Simeon did not interrupt her for a time.

Finally, after a good while had passed, so had the king.

Jenny, the king is gone, Simeon told her. *You became so distracted wondering what might happen, or what could happen, or what should happen, that you didn't notice him go right past you.*

She knew he was telling her the truth because as she cautiously turned her head to look behind her, she caught sight of Judah. He was running across the field to where she was stashed between the rocks; the look on his face was dreadful.

"Jennifer," he whispered sharply. "Don't EVER run ahead like that again … the king could have seen you!" Judah was furious with her and although she couldn't blame him, she also couldn't help it.

"Simeon told me to go," she said sheepishly. It seemed the more she followed her Shailma, the more it upset the other Travelers.

Instead of getting into an argument with her brother—or anyone else who was beginning to lecture her—Jennifer decided to tell them about the crack she'd found between the rocks. With any luck, such good news would help them forget they were angry with her.

"I had some time to find a way in," she said. She meant it as a joke to lighten the mood, but no one laughed. "Look here," she continued. "If we can wiggle behind this one rock, there's a large crack in the side of the cave. I've been looking at it and I think we should be able to squeeze through."

"We would certainly be well hidden, and it's where we need to get to open the maps," Pierce said. He sounded almost pleased with Jennifer but refused to say so.

"Yes, I think you have found the way inside," Bella said. "Nice job, J. But don't ever run ahead like that again, do you hear? You nearly gave me a heart attack!"

Jennifer didn't wish to argue, so she simply said, "OK, Bella. I'm sorry." The fact was that she was not sorry at all. If she had not obeyed Simeon and ran to the crevice between the rocks, none of them would have taken the time to look long enough to find the way inside. They would have gone another way altogether. Even if they did take a peek inside the crevice, it would have been only briefly, and the way inside would have been missed.

Simeon knew what he was doing after all. She was safe, and they had a way inside. One by one they squeezed behind the gigantic boulder that had been rolled in front of the cave. One by one they pushed their way through the side of the cave that had been broken down. Before long, they were all standing wide-eyed inside the darkness of the Carphlour Caves.

"I forgot this cave was filled with those horrible red-tailed spiders," Jennifer moped.

"I doubt we'll need any of those on this trip," Sam replied.

"We have no time to waste," Bella announced. "Pierce, lay out the maps … quickly!" Pierce had already begun doing exactly that, and as one particular map sprang to life, the other closed itself up. Pierce opened it again and laid it on the cold floor, but the moment his hands let go, it folded itself up.

"Well, I guess we won't be needing that map," Matt stated.

"Let's hope not," spouted Pierce.

While they all stood hunched around the map that was moaning and groaning and shaking and sputtering, Sam had moved to the corner closest to the crack in the side of the wall. He needed as much light as he could find if he was going to scan through the Book of Lies and the Book of Truths.

The boy was determined to learn as much as he could from the books. He squatted on the floor, squinted, and began reading; mumbling really, as he quietly whispered the words from the books as quickly as he could. He tried stuffing his brain full, memorizing points and statements, in case there was no time to pull the books out later when their words might be needed.

It was a brilliant idea, too, and his Shailma helped Sam remember much of what he was reading. He could see it going into his mind as though he was watching the book be re-written on his brain.

Sam knew the more words he could read aloud, the more would be written inside of his mind, so he read quickly.

What Sam did not know, was that he wasn't the only one listening to the words from the Book of Truths and the Book of Lies. Without his awareness, the Dark Deceivers had moved in close and they too, were listening to the words and twisting them before they could be pulled into Sam's mind.

The Dark Deceivers were adding more lies so that the words would become completely mixed-up if he tried to retrieve them. They would undoubtedly cause the Travelers much more harm than they would provide protection which, of course, was the Dark Deceivers' plan all along.

Chapter 15

Unknown Places

Squeals and gasps arose from both Jennifer and Bella as they were hovering over the map, taking it all in. Much of the usual rigmarole was there; valleys that dug themselves down deep and water that began to rush. There were countless armies, although they seemed confused and angry, and then in the far east, there was a swarm of the large, clawed flying creatures that had tried to grab Jennifer on the last journey.

She felt the shoulder of her cloak where the clawed flying savages had ripped it, and she was delighted to feel that the cloak had been strangely restored.

"Odd," she whispered.

There were some other unusual agitations which also stirred on the map. These were the particular things the girls were musing about. Kaija Mae and Sam suddenly hollered from two different spaces across the cave.

"What is it?" Kaija Mae asked.

"What's that map up to?" Sam shouted.

Kaija Mae headed toward the map, but Sam stayed where he was and did not take his eyes off of the words in the Book of Truths that he was packing into his memory.

"Come and look," Jennifer shouted.

"Everyone," Bella added. "Come!" They were jumping and squealing wildly, so everyone rushed over—except Sam—hoping their eyes were finding good things.

Sadly, their eyes found nothing good to fall on. What they were witnessing was the slow but steady destruction of the Dark Land. Now, the Travelers hated the land. Oh, how they hated it. They hated the vesta beetles and the cradle bugs. They hated the vexaturs and especially the traps and the Dark Deceivers and the evil deception of it all. They hated both the king and the Trows deeply. Most of all, they hated the curse.

They were not especially fond of Miriam either, although they had not yet figured out just how evil she truly was. But for now, the dark-haired Traveler had not come with them, and as far as any of them knew, she had stayed back in the hollow. Oh, if only that was where that wretched girl had remained, things might not have gotten as bad as they were about to get.

The complete demolition of Trilleah would have made them immensely happy. That is, of course, IF they were not actually in the clutches of the land … and IF they had already freed the souls of the Waiting Ones. But with so many souls—their loved ones especially—still cursed to the forest, the destruction of Trilleah was not anything to hope for or rejoice about; not yet.

"What IS that?" Judah asked. Even though he was still a good distance from the map, he could see bits and pieces that were being hurled upward. It looked like the chipping away of rocks. Hard chunks were being thrown from the map and were landing on the floor with a *thud.*

The Travelers stepped back to keep themselves from getting hit with any of the flying debris but not back so far they couldn't see what was going on in the midst of the Living Maps. It was wretched.

"It looks like a war zone over there," Matt said. He pointed to the side that was hurling the stone debris. Small fires were beginning to erupt on the other side of the map, close to their hollow, and it looked as though a spark had landed just outside the rock that covered its entrance, igniting a bit of a fire.

"We have to hurry!" Bella shrieked. As they waited without patience for the map to draw them a path, they began chattering away about the time, the day, the sun, and mostly the gate and how it had been broken down.

"Ouch," Matt said as he quickly ducked. Not quickly enough, however, as a good-sized chunk of debris was launched up and caught him right on the cheek.

Jennifer suddenly blurted out a thought with great wisdom—or tomfoolery perhaps—coming from somewhere she didn't know.

"Wait a minute!" she demanded. "If the gates are broken, wouldn't that mean they can't close when the sun tucks itself behind the horizon?" That got the attention of everyone, even Matt, who was still rubbing the big red spot on his cheek.

"It seems to me, and maybe this is my own version of common sense, but it seems to me that if the gates are broken and cannot close since they have crumbled to the ground, that we have as much time as we need inside the gates," she said excitedly.

"It seems to me," Judah added with a grin, "that you may be right."

"It seems to me," Pierce said, "that the map has drawn its path. LOOK!" he shouted.

They all looked; everyone except for Sam, who was still on the far side of the cave shoving his mind full with every word that was written in the precious books he held. "I trust you to figure it out," he hollered without taking his eyes off of the pages.

Sure enough. The path had been drawn, and it raised no hope in anyone who was seeing it. Where the path wanted to lead them was straight into the heart of the land—a place they had never journeyed to before and knew nothing about. Jennifer had heard about it once or twice from her Shailma and had repeated what she'd been told to Bella, but her auntie refused to believe anything about it.

"It's too horrid," Bella would say. "It simply cannot be true that something so hellish could exist … even in Trilleah," she argued. "I worry about you, J. Your mind is so deep and imaginable that even the unimaginable seems to find space there." Jennifer's feelings were a little hurt by the doubt that came from her auntie, but she knew what Simeon had told her and nothing Bella could say would make her doubt her Shailma.

Her mind was brought right back to this instant as her auntie continued to whine. "We can't go there," Bella repeated.

"Why not?" Jennifer wanted to know. If Bella hadn't believed what Jennifer had told her about the center of Trilleah, then she should have no problem journeying there if that was where the map was leading.

Whether Bella had believed her or not made no difference now, however. Again, Jennifer's naivety was allowing great braveness to rise in her. "If the path is leading us there, doesn't it make sense that we should follow it?"

"I suppose," Bella said, even though she had a bad feeling in her belly about where the path was leading. "It's so far from where we are is all. I understand now why the Shailmas didn't want to bring us back until Summer Solstice; it's a long journey to the center of Trilleah."

"I'm not sure I trust the maps anymore," Pierce interrupted the conversation.

"They've been off lately, especially with the Labyrinth," Matt added. "Shouldn't the map have known about that?" he asked.

The debate went on for a long time until Pierce ended it abruptly.

"The path has been drawn," he said. "We are going to follow it precisely and trust that it knows what it needs to know." He scratched his head and was obviously nervous about such a decision, but he knew someone had to make it, so he decided it might as well be him.

"We have no other choice," he said, and everyone agreed.

He looked at the map one last time, to be sure he had all of the turns and curves and roundabouts straightened out in his mind before picking up the map at one corner. The map immediately folded itself up and allowed Pierce to tuck it into his cloak.

"Let's go," he mumbled. "Sam, put the books away; it's time to go." Sam grunted to show his concern but closed the books nevertheless, and tucked them inside his cloak.

The Travelers each disappeared inside their hoods, and one by one squeezed back through the side of the cave, past the small crevice, and out into the wide open land of darkness. They would no longer be able to tell where the king was, or if he was moving in their direction, since the entire land was rumbling and shaking fiercely. Certainly, Shrailzhar's movements would be undetectable amidst such a ruckus.

"Everyone, stay together," Pierce shouted, and everyone did.

They wandered this way and that, ducking debris and trying to shield their eyes from the dirt that was swirling around them. Nobody spoke to another, but everyone was deep in silent conversation with their Shailmas.

Simeon, what's happening? Will we find the tablet? Both maybe? The land is throwing itself at us.

He answered none of her questions, but only reminded her to have hope, trust him, and carry on.

Jennifer felt like she'd been swallowed up by the Dark Land and all she wanted to do was get out. She took a big breath and held it as they walked and ducked and jumped over holes in the ground that were getting bigger and bigger. All the while the land continued to shake and rumble and break apart.

The sky continued tearing itself up and small bits of it were starting to fall to the ground.

"Judah, where are you?" she squealed. As much as she was trying to trust Simeon, Jennifer was still deeply afraid and needed the one person she trusted most to be near her. She wished and begged and pleaded with Simeon to show himself to her, but she knew that no amount of such tactics would work. The Shailma showed himself only when he decided to show himself. Nothing would persuade him otherwise.

"Over here, Jelly Bean," she heard. Judah was just behind her, so she slowed down to wait for him. As soon as he was beside her, she grabbed his arm. He squeezed her hand.

"It's OK, no worries right?" How did he sound so confident? She wished she was as confident as her brother, although she knew that deep down inside, Judah was not confident at all.

"No worries," she answered back. Her voice was racked with fear and cracked as she spoke.

"Over there!" Pierce shouted. They all looked to where "over there" might be. They did not like what they saw. A large slough was raging, swirling around and around like it was in a blender. The filthy water was splashing up at the edges, and the roar coming from it was tremendous. It sounded like a hundred angry waterfalls arguing with one another.

As they drew closer, they saw that the slough did not hold water, as one might expect. No; this was a slough filled with blood. Or, at least it had enough blood in it to overpower the water and turn it into blood.

"Where did *this* come from?" Judah screamed, horrified.

"It was on the map, didn't you see it?" Pierce asked, puzzled. "How did you not see it?" he questioned. Pierce sounded angry, but then again, that was not an unusual tone for him. And of course, coming upon a large slough of furiously churning blood didn't exactly help his disposition!

Bella covered her ears and cried. "Oh dear," she repeated over and over and over again. All of her words seemed to disappear except for those two. She must have said them a hundred times.

"Bella, stop!" Pierce finally said. She was getting everyone more panicked than they needed to be, although panic certainly seemed to be necessary at the moment.

The closer they came, the more the smell sickened their bellies.

"Where is this from?" Judah wondered.

"Pierce, there's a bridge. Are we to go over it or around it?" Sam asked. He was so busy repeating (under his breath) the words he'd read that he couldn't focus on anything else. Besides that, he hadn't gotten a look at the map, so Sam was completely dependent upon the others. He barely seemed to notice what the rest wished they could ignore.

"We go around, according to the map," Pierce answered. They had now reached the shore of the bloody slough, and their noses were burning with a terrible smell of death.

Simeon, Jennifer wondered, *what is all this blood from?* She waited and followed mindlessly those who were leading her. *Simeon?* She asked again in her mind, although a bit louder. Without him responding, she briefly wondered if he'd left her. While she was so deeply listening for the calming voice of her Shailma, it was another voice she heard.

Jennifer, Simeon has gone. He led you to this place to leave you here. He is a jokester. A bully. A liar. A monster. A traitor. He's led you here, they all led you here to this very place, to leave you. The Shailmas are not real, you foolish, foolish girl.

Her eyes grew large and her stomach churned. She listened as the unfamiliar voice went on and on and on. Finally, the words which Jennifer could not bear to hear, came to her.

Simeon is dead.

All the Shailmas are dead.

This is the blood of the Shailmas.

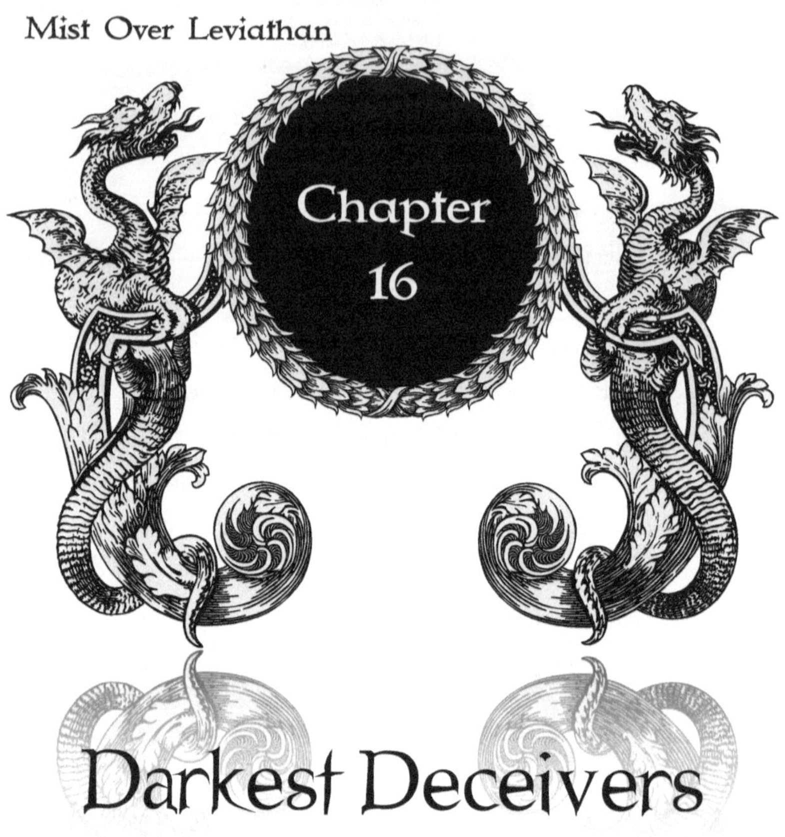

Darkest Deceivers

"No!" she screamed. Jennifer didn't even care that the word was loud outside of her mind … or that everyone else stopped suddenly and turned to look at her.

"What is it, J?" Bella questioned.

"Oh, Bella," she sobbed and slumped to the ground. Bella ran to her and Judah knelt beside his sister.

"What is it, J?" they both shrieked. Jennifer was weeping so hard that she couldn't catch her breath or tell them what she'd heard. She didn't realize that it was the Dark Deceivers who had filled her head with such brutally cruel lies. They had so filled her mind, in fact, that she stopped trying to listen for Simeon. Of course, this only gave them more power to whisper whatever lies they thought would be the most damaging.

A few moments of her weeping and wailing dragged past, and finally, Pierce had completely run out of patience.

"Jennifer!" he demanded. Bella shot him a horrible look and elbowed him in the ribs.

"Pierce," she whispered, but he refused to acknowledge her annoyance and continued speaking harshly to the girl crumpled and weeping on the ground.

"Pull yourself together and tell us what happened, this instant. We don't have time for this foolishness," he scolded.

Bella held her breath. She knew such harshness would not prove to work well with her niece. She breathed a sigh of relief, however, when she turned out to be wrong. Jennifer caught her breath and sniffled. She wiped her nose with the back of her hand and sat up. Bella was puzzled.

"Pierce ... I was searching for my Shailma." ✳ *Sniffles* ✳ "But it wasn't Simeon that came to me." ✳ *A few more sniffles* ✳ "I heard horrible things, Pierce. Wretched things!" The sniffles turned into sobs once again, and once again Pierce had no patience for such nonsense.

"Jennifer!" he said sharply. "Stop it."

Maybe it was the sharpness that caught the broken girl's attention, but nonetheless, her attention was caught. She stood up, breathed deeply, and determined in herself to tell Pierce—and the others—what she'd heard. And she did. Without any sobs or sniffles or delays, Jennifer proceeded to repeat word for word what was told to her mind.

"… and this is the blood of our Shailmas." As she repeated outside of her mind what had been played inside of it, she heard the complete nonsense of it all and knew instantly—before anyone else had the chance to tell her—that she'd been deceived.

She wasn't sure anyone else would have known she'd been deceived, but now, it sounded like such hogwash that she was embarrassed to think she had believed it for even a moment. Jennifer was even more embarrassed as she considered the unruly scene she had just displayed in front of the others.

Even as she was considering all of these things, the Dark Deceivers were continuing to flood her mind with similar rubbish because after all, Dark Deceivers are not ones to easily give up. They continued on and on until suddenly Jennifer remembered what Simeon had told her about the weapons she needed to fight this war.

In a loud voice, and not caring who might hear and think her crazy, Jennifer spoke words of truth. She opened her mouth and the words powerfully—ferociously, even—poured out.

"Indeed, our Shailmas ARE with us always, to the ends of the earth and this is not even CLOSE to the ends of the earth."

Sure enough, everyone began rolling their eyes and looking at the girl as though she'd smacked her head when she collapsed and rattled her brains around but good. She didn't care. At that moment, she cared much more about setting the Dark Deceivers straight and making them flee, than what the other Travelers might think of her. She'd explain it to them later, but for now, she was intent on battling these Dark Deceivers with the weapons Simeon had taught her to use.

"Simeon is here with me now. He hasn't left me, and all things are as they must be and it must be that he is here. It makes no difference if my mind can hear him or not hear him—that does NOT determine if he stays with me or not. Truth is truth, no matter what the circumstances may seem.

"Now, you Dark Deceivers of evil, I am telling you that you are liars and there is no truth in you. I am binding you up and throwing you all out of my mind. I am giving you notice that since I have bound you up, you may not go and bother or harass anyone else here either. You are bound and without any power. The Shailmas are beacons of light and peace and truth. They are truth, and you are not, so BE GONE!"

Jennifer didn't realize that by this time, she was shouting at the top of her lungs. She didn't notice that all the Travelers had gathered around her, enclosing her in a circle of themselves, nor did she see that the Dark Deceivers had exited her mind … but the others saw it.

They watched, fascinated and in awe of such power and authority over the Dark Deceivers. They had watched with their own eyes as many dark shadowy figures exited through her ears and darted quickly, disappearing into the sky. They had noticed that the Dark Deceivers were each bound in chains and that they were all bound together. Not even one could remain behind or escape to return later.

The Dark Deceivers squirmed and floundered and thrashed about as they exited through Jennifer's ears but could not wiggle free from the chains that had them shackled together. Jennifer may not have been able to see what the others had seen, but she felt it and shuddered. From the bottom of her feet—which were hot inside the ugly boots—to the top of her head—which no longer was hidden under the cloak hood —she shuddered. When the shuddering ended, so did the horrible sounds and words and voices that had been filling her mind.

It was quiet … altogether quiet in her mind except for one small, still voice—Simeon.

I am here, Little One, he whispered so gently to her. *I never left you, not even for a moment. I am with you always.*

I couldn't hear you, Simeon. I got afraid. I'm sorry, she cried in the depths of her mind. It dawned on her that she had opened the door to let the Dark Deceivers in the very moment that she doubted Simeon. The battle had begun when she thought he had left her. *I am so sorry I doubted you, Simeon,* she silently cried. *I remembered what you told me about using my weapons of truth and words. I remembered.*

Yes, you did, he said, and although Jennifer couldn't see him with her natural eyes, she knew he was smiling at her from within. *I'm proud of you, Jenny. You battled them and you won. You can be trusted, Little One. You can be trusted.*

Simeon, I know you were helping me. I know I didn't do any of that on my own, though. My words are without any power. But you, Simeon, I know it was you who put the words in my mouth and who gave me the power to speak them out. Thank you, Simeon, thank you.

You're welcome, he replied gently. *Now let's get moving. Time is valuable ... and short.* This reminded her of what she'd thought earlier about the gates crumbling, and it made her wonder; if the gates could no longer close themselves, why was time still important? She didn't ask Simeon; she felt she'd bothered him enough for the time being. Nevertheless, he answered her.

Jennifer, time is valuable—while you are correct in understanding the gates can no longer be closed, you have forgotten the land is crumbling. The king is working to destroy his kingdom; you don't want to be inside on that final day of destruction.

Drat! She was annoyed that she hadn't even thought of such an obvious thing. She wasted no more time wondering about such things.

"Let's go," she said loudly and began to push her way through the Travelers, who continued to circle her and be in shock at what they had just heard and witnessed. Jennifer moved quickly, even though nobody else seemed to move at all.

"Are you coming?" she shouted back to them. Judah looked at Bella, and Pierce looked at Sam, and Matt looked at Judah, and round and round they went. Not one of them had words to describe what they'd just seen, but from the looks that each one wore on their faces, it was evident they had all seen the same thing.

"Hey," Jennifer shouted again. "COME ON!"

Finally, they got their feet moving, realizing that now was not the time to discuss the event. They knew what they'd seen, and each had a new respect for the little girl who was already far in front of them on the path. As much as Pierce hated having anyone else lead, he knew that she was indeed the leader—and was reasonably content to allow it.

The Travelers plugged their noses as they passed the slough of blood; it was a sickening smell. Once they reached the other side,

Jennifer seemed confident in where she was headed. Pierce watched carefully, however, to ensure she stayed close to the path the map had drawn for them in the Carphlour Caves.

The farther they wandered, the calmer the land became.

"Probably because we're getting farther and farther away from the edges," Matt said. "Remember, the king is destroying the land from the outside in."

As they discussed what they'd seen with Jennifer earlier, they failed to pay as much attention as they needed to. That is, until Jennifer stopped short. She held her arms up as if the general of a large army. Everyone stopped. Nobody moved because nobody knew why she had stopped and was now standing still with her arms outstretched.

Some tried to look ahead to see what she was seeing, but mostly the Travelers kept their eyes focused on the back of her cloak, watching for her to move. They determined to stay as still as Jennifer did, for as long as she did. It wasn't long at all, however. After only a few moments, Jennifer screamed.

"RUN!!" she wailed and began running herself. Nobody had to be told twice. The instant she moved her feet, every Traveler moved theirs too. As fast as they could without going past the girl, they ran.

Not even one took the time to look around and nobody slowed down. They had no idea why they were running, or where they were going, but they were determined to get there quickly. Finally, out of breath and out of time, Jennifer dove into a small opening just beneath a large boulder. Everyone followed.

Inside, and all piled on the ground, they breathed heavily. It took a few minutes for some to catch their breath, but as soon as they did, the obvious questions were asked.

"What did you see?"

"Why were we running?"

"Where are we?"

Question after question was blurted out until finally, Jennifer hushed them all.

"Please," she wheezed, "I can't answer everything at once!" She suddenly knew how they felt when her questions came by the dozen.

"Where are we?" Matt asked first.

"I have no idea," she answered honestly. "I was following Simeon, and this is where he led me. I would wonder if I heard him wrong, except the opening to this hollow was exactly where he said it was. If it wasn't, I guess I would have cracked my head right open with flinging myself into the boulder …"

"Thank goodness he led you," Bella said.

"Why were we running?" Sam asked next. "What did you see?" This was indeed the question everyone had been waiting for an answer to, so there were no interruptions as she opened her mouth to try and offer one.

Chapter 17

No Way Out

"I was following where Simeon told me to go, which I think was close to the path that was drawn on the map," Jennifer explained. "Then I noticed a little to the left, some of the king's army." Her eyes grew large as she was telling of what she'd seen. The others moved a little closer so they didn't miss even the smallest detail.

"They were not on foot, I'm afraid," she whispered as though the army might hear her. "They were riding on the backs of enormous beasts that looked a lot like the beast we saw King Shrailzhar sitting on."

"Remember? With the cradle bugs?" Jennifer wasn't sure why the Travelers were looking at her so strangely. Either they didn't remember the gigantic beast on which the king was riding that day, or they thought she was crazy.

The Travelers looked away from her—and at each other—and wondered how they had missed such a thing. How did they miss the army riding on those beasts and yet Jennifer had seen them? They were all thinking the same thing, although nobody said it out loud.

Jennifer continued, unable to read their thoughts.

"When I was beneath the ground, in the adder's pit, I saw many of these dreadful beasts." Now the Travelers looked straight at her for they knew nothing of the adder's pit she was talking about or what she had seen under the ground or anything that had happened when the vines had pulled her below.

In fact, the only thing they knew about any of it was that Jennifer had been removed—somewhat safely, but tragically—by her Shailma. The week after she was returned to Westlock, all of the Travelers had received a message from Bella telling them she had been returned home and, *although she's back, she's in bad shape*, Bella had told them.

The Travelers hadn't heard much else about Jennifer or her ordeal, but now and then Bella did send a short message to each of them, updating that she was improving slowly. Nothing had been said about an adder's pit or beasts or anything else that went on there so now, with such words spilling from Jennifer's lips, they were all in a bit of a confusion.

"We didn't know," Pierce said.

"That's because I never told you," Jennifer replied.

"Regardless, I am telling you that I was in the adder's pit which turns out, is the king's throne room." She rolled her eyes because the Travelers' awkward stares were frustrating her. "I saw these beasts there, and now here, I saw them coming after us" Jennifer pointed to where they had just come in from and shivered.

With all the eyes still glued to her, she continued. "In the adder's pit, they could come nowhere near me because of the circle of Shailmas that surrounded me." She was talking as though everybody knew what she was referring to. None did, of course, but no one interrupted. They sat on the floor, knee to knee, and listened closely, amazed that Jennifer had made it out of such a horrific place at all.

"There's no way you should have come out of there," Sam blurted out.

"I know," she said quietly. "But I did."

There was a moment of quiet as the reality of such a miracle sunk into everyone's mind. Soon, Jennifer continued with her description of the beasts she'd seen; the entire group could hardly believe anything she said, though. It was so outrageously unbelievable.

"They have huge wings," she explained, stretching her arms out wide in front of her. "Although nothing like our Shailmas' wings."

"Um, you've seen a Shailma's wings?" Sam asked. He leaned in closer, making Jennifer uncomfortable. His eyes were as large as saucers now.

As soon as he asked the question, Jennifer realized that not everyone had seen the things she'd seen, nor heard the things she'd heard, nor experienced some of what she'd experienced since coming to Trilleah. Not everyone had constant communication with their Shailmas like she had, so trying to explain such things suddenly seemed unimportant and, well, unexplainable.

"OK, well let me assure you that these beasts are a hundred times more beastly than the one Shrailzhar was on that day when the cradle bugs skinned it alive," she said.

"Anyway," Jennifer continued, "they were behind us, and I noticed them at the same time they noticed me. The only thing we could do was run. When Simeon told me about this hollow, there was nothing to do other than dive inside."

The Travelers had been listening intently, but now they had a thousand questions. One seemed as important as any other and all apparently needed answers—immediately.

"Did Simeon mention how we are supposed to get out of here?" Bella asked.

"Ya," Sam said. "It seems reasonable to think that those beasts you were describing will be waiting for us out there."

"Now we're trapped in here," Matt said.

"Wait, everybody!" Jennifer said, waving her hands wildly to get the attention of everyone—and to stop the questioning. "Don't think such things. Simeon would not lead us IN TO somewhere we cannot get OUT OF. There is a way out; there has to be. We just have to find it," she sighed, "or wait for the Shailmas to lead us out."

Jennifer pushed herself up from the floor; the others followed. They knew Jennifer had something they did not have—even though they didn't know what that thing was—and were suddenly confident in following her.

They began moving slowly along the walls, looking for another way out. They dared not even peek out of the entrance which they'd slipped through just in case whatever it was that was following them was still out there … waiting.

Sam went back through all the words he could recall from the Book of Truths and the Book of Lies, but nothing came to his mind that seemed to apply here. All he could do was what everyone else was doing—search desperately for a way out. They ran their hands along the walls hoping to find a crack or a hole. They found nothing of the sort in that main chamber.

This was not a large hollow like Asphelia's was, but there were a couple of small, dark passageways. Nobody particularly wanted to venture down them, however, but after checking every crevice of the main chamber, those dark passageways seemed their only hope.

"I think we should all stay together," Bella answered when Judah asked who wanted to try heading down the bigger passageway with him.

"You're right," Judah said. "Let's go together."

Even though it was the biggest of the passageways, it was still quite small. One by one they went in single file and searched for any gaps or openings that might be secret doors or hidden passageways.

Nothing.

They found nothing and it was getting cramped in the small passageway. Murmuring and whispering started about whether to keep going or turn back and try the other one. Judah suggested they go to the very end of this one before turning back.

But then, close to the end of the passageway when there seemed nowhere else to go but back, Pierce saw a dim light just below his feet. He stopped suddenly, causing Bella to bump into the back of him.

"Oaf," she grunted as her face ran straight into his scratchy cloak. "Why are you stopping?" she asked, obviously frustrated.

"Look down," he said.

She did, and soon both of them began kicking at the dirt with their feet. Jennifer also heard Pierce say to look down, so she did. There was a tiny sliver of light under her feet as well, and Judah's and Sam's and Matt's. Soon they were all kicking at the dirt frantically trying to see where this light was coming from—and where it might lead. Hope began to well up from somewhere inside each of the Travelers.

"Here," Kaija Mae spoke up. "Would these help?" she asked. There in her hand were two long, jagged rocks with a sharp point on one end of each. They looked a little like daggers, and she handed one to Pierce and another to Judah.

"Um, YES!" they hollered.

"Where did you get these?" Sam asked.

"I saw them in the Carphlour Caves and thought they might come in handy," she said, quite proud of herself at the moment. "I never thought we'd be clawing our way through a dirt floor in the back of some hollow, but it seems ..." She never finished her sentence. Before she could get the last of her words out, the boys had broken through the ground.

Below them was exactly what they'd been looking for—a way out. At least, hopefully, it was a way out. "It doesn't look safe," Bella complained.

"It looks safer than going back out the way we came in," Kaija Mae replied.

"I suppose," Bella answered.

"I'll go down first," Judah suggested. "If I can wiggle my way through the opening, I'll see what's down there and maybe it will lead us out the back."

"Be careful, Judah. Please!" Jennifer whined. She needed her brother now more than ever and did not want to think about the possibilities of losing him through a crack in the hollow ground.

"Maybe Pierce could go first," she said.

"Why should I go first?" Pierce stammered.

What Jennifer wanted to say was, "Because I don't really like you. Because if YOU disappear ... or get eaten by something dreadful ... or if it leads you right back out to where those beasts are waiting, then they can skin YOU alive instead of my brother." That's what she wanted to say, but she never said any of those things.

What she did say was nowhere near what was in her heart.

"I just know you like to go first because you are so brave, Pierce," is what she really said, even though it pained her greatly to say something so ridiculous. She noticed Bella looking at her oddly and Jennifer wasted no time in rolling her eyes and giving her aunt an excessively dramatic look.

"I'll go," Judah said quietly. "I'm very brave also, Jelly Bean." He winked at her, and she knew that he was aware she'd only said what was required for the situation, and not what she truly felt in her heart.

"I know," she whispered, and even though she tried to sound confident, it came out as sadness. "Be careful, Judah."

"Always am," he answered. Well, she knew that to be untrue but trusted that he would be careful this time and that Shemaiah would be with him as well.

A few wiggles and twists and turns, and Judah was deep into the crevasse they had opened up. Pierce got down on his belly and stuck his face into the hole.

"What do you see?" he shouted.

They waited for an answer but heard nothing.

"Judah," Pierce shouted a bit louder. "Does it lead out? Judah … JUDAH!"

When they heard nothing from Judah for those few seconds, panic began to set in amongst the group. They gazed at one another with looks of horror spreading across each face. The panic was halted as the voice of Judah was heard clearly, moments later.

"Hey, I think there's a way out down here," he shouted back up to them.

They began laughing, but it was a nervous laugh. It was finally Matt who spoke. "This isn't funny, but I have to laugh so I don't cry." One laugh ignited another and so on and so forth. Soon, all of the Travelers who were surrounding the small gap in the ground and staring down into a space that they hoped would take them out, were laughing … hard … so hard that their bellies began to hurt. They didn't care.

"Hey," Judah said as he popped his head back up into the middle of the group. "What's so funny?"

He startled them, and the laughing stopped suddenly, only to be ignited all over again as they looked at Judah, who had grime smeared over his face and in his hair. "You look like a gopher in your hole," Sam said between gasps, which only made the Travelers laugh harder for that was exactly what Judah looked like.

Now, it didn't seem an appropriate time for such belly-aching laughter, but then again, perhaps it was a perfect time. They felt safe in this hollow. The shaking of the land seemed to have slowed for the time-being, and they had found an escape from their cage.

It made Judah remember a time when his daddy was still with them. He remembered how his daddy used to say to Mamma, "Sometimes in the worst of situations, the best thing to do is laugh. After all, why not?" Judah recalled how his mamma and daddy used to laugh a lot. He greatly missed their laughter. He suddenly had a drive in his belly to collect the rest of the clay tablets—no matter how difficult —and break the curse that was holding his mamma.

"Oh dear," Bella sighed, holding her belly. It was aching terribly now from so much laughter. "We really must get out of here," she exclaimed as she tried to catch her breath and control her laughing.

"Judah, is there a way out down there? Did you see anything?" Matt hollered down the hole since Judah had disappeared again.

"It looks like it," he shouted back to them.

"Is there room for us to all come down or just one at a time?" Pierce shouted down the hole. They didn't have to wait this time for an answer.

"There's plenty of space. Come down and let's get out of here." His answer came floating back up into the passageway and sounded like the best of answers to the Travelers' ears.

"Jennifer, you go first. Kaija Mae and Bella, you go next," Pierce began instructing. The girls didn't mind that he was taking control of the situation; even Jennifer, who normally wanted to do the opposite of what Pierce said just to annoy the boy. Such rebellion was not her normal attitude, but there was just something about that boy that got under her skin.

Not this time, however. Since the air was getting rather thin in the small passageway and they were beginning to feel crowded—like trapped animals—Pierce didn't have to give the directions twice. Jennifer immediately put her legs down through the crevasse. Judah helped her jump down, for it was a long way to fall.

The cloaks made the decent more difficult, but they dared not remove them after the episode with Matt a couple of journeys ago when he'd been sucked into a trap of the king. The cloaks could be quite a nuisance, to be sure, but the necessity of them overshadowed any nuisance they could be.

One by one the Travelers made their way down through the crevice and into the space below. There was much more light in that space, and it did look like it was coming from somewhere not too far away. They hurried as quickly as they could toward the light and were delighted when they saw the large opening they were coming up to.

As the Travelers came closer to the mouth of the cave, Pierce spoke up, stating the obvious and annoying the others … as he usually did.

"Don't just go darting out into the open," he shouted.

Judah, who was at the front hollered back. "Of course not!" Then he turned to Jennifer, who was still right behind him. "What kind of idiot does he think I am?" he muttered.

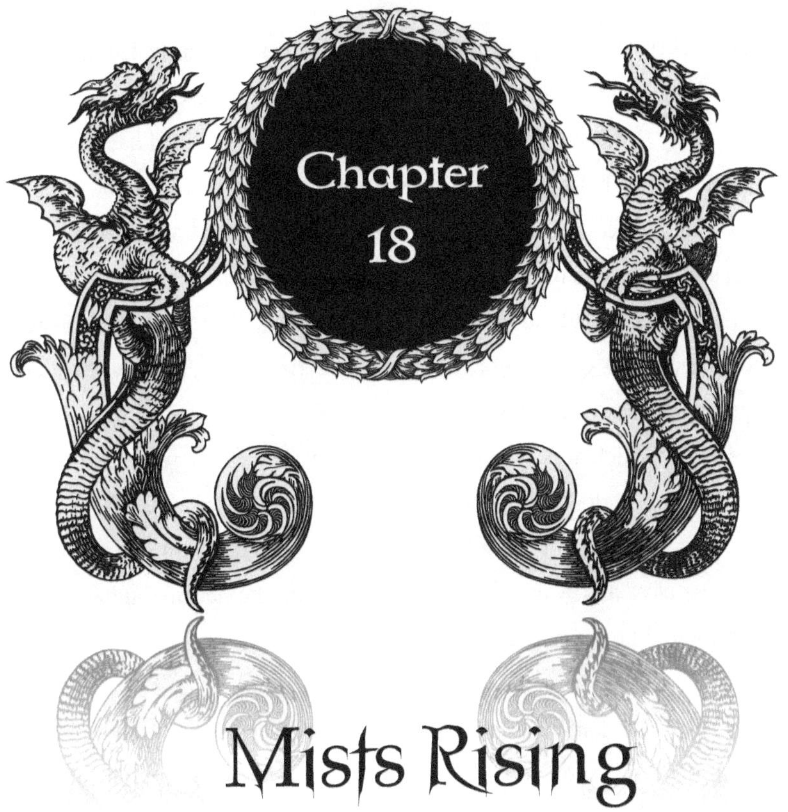

Chapter 18

Mists Rising

"I wonder if our own hollow is also a cave such as this one?" Judah wondered to Jennifer. She shrugged but knew her brother couldn't see her gesture under the heavy cloak. "I bet it is," he continued. Jennifer didn't care one way or other and didn't bother to answer him.

They arrived at the mouth of the cave and stopped. Judah peered out and saw nothing out of the ordinary, which for Trilleah, where even the unordinary was ordinary, was quite a task. He saw no sign of the army or anything like Jennifer had been describing, so they cautiously snuck out of the cave and into the open. The land had calmed itself, but not before shaking apart a great portion of rocks and trees. The rips in the sky had become bigger as well, revealing more of the blackness that was moving in to swallow the Dark Land.

Judah had no idea which way to go. The path they were supposed to be on had not included wandering through a hollow and coming out a cave clear on the other side.

"Which way, Pierce?" he asked as the group was now once again huddled closely together.

"I … I don't know," Pierce said. They had no time to go back into the cave and wait for the maps again, and he became agitated. "I don't know how far around this stupid hollow took us," he bellyached. "Can anyone see something familiar?"

"Familiar?" Bella burst out. "Is that a serious question because if so, it's a ridiculous one!" she stated. Pierce was in no mood for her attitude and was about to lash out and remind everyone that he was trying his best to get them back to the path without any help from anyone, and so forth and whatnot, but he didn't get far in his tongue-lashing because Sam spoke first.

"That does!" he shrieked. They looked to where he was pointing and saw, to their dismay, that they had gone directly underneath the bloody slough. The smell alone should have told them where they were.

"Oh bother," Bella bellyached. "We didn't get far at all!" She coughed and covered her nose … the smell was hideous.

"We sort of did, Bella," Jennifer said. "The path was trying to lead us to this side of the slough, except it led us *around* it instead of *under* it. It seems we are right where we are supposed to be!"

"I guess you're right," Bella replied, still sounding frustrated about not being farther on the journey, and still covering her nose.

They were hushed since they didn't know where the army had gone or if they were still waiting on the back side of the slough. A great bluish-gray mist had come up and covered the land so it was difficult to see very far in any direction. That was probably a good thing. If they couldn't see the Army of Trilleah, then the Army of Trilleah could not see them. At least, that was their hope.

"Let's go," Pierce whispered. "This way," he pointed and began walking ahead of the rest. They didn't run now, though. They were hunched down, hiding amongst the mist and sneaking in their most sneaky manner possible.

The Travelers slinked around this bush and tiptoed over that hole. They ducked under low branches and broken shreds of the sky that had fallen and gotten caught up in the trees. All the while, they kept their eyes open for the Army of Shrailzhar. So far, there was no sign of them. However, with the mist getting thicker and lower, seeing much of anything was becoming precariously difficult.

The land seemed still, with nothing falling from the sky above and the ground staying firm below. Maybe the king had changed his mind and decided not to destroy Trilleah after all. They could only hope this was the truth.

Of course, it was not.

They had found their way back to what seemed like that path the maps had drawn earlier and were careful to stay on it. Pierce was in front leading the way. The way to where, nobody knew. Unfortunately, the further they journeyed, the thicker the mist became until they could barely see at all.

Bella grabbed the back of Pierce and Jennifer grabbed the back of Bella and so forth and so on until the Travelers had formed one attached single-file line. They all hoped deeply that Pierce had some idea of where he was headed or that maybe, by some freak chance, or miraculous happenstance, he could see into the mist better than they could. He couldn't, of course, but just kept putting one foot in front of the other, carefully and slowly. "I hope the army can't see through the mist better than we can because we'll never be able to see them until they are right upon us ..."

Bella heard him, but her mind formed no words to say, so her mouth said nothing. She had closed her eyes a few steps back, since she couldn't see anyway, and was simply trusting Pierce—and Shura. More Shura than Pierce at the moment, she decided.

"Bella," Jennifer whispered. "What's that over to the left?" she asked. Now Bella was forced to open her eyes and look to the left. She squinted hard.

"I see nothing, J. Are you sure you're not just imagining things?"

"You see nothing at all?" Jennifer sounded surprised.

"Not a thing," Bella replied. Jennifer wondered then, how it was that she could see because there was no doubt that she saw something.

She squinted and tried harder to focus and make out what it was, but couldn't. They kept following Pierce, who was leading them closer and closer to a bottomless looking sea.

Surely there cannot be an entire sea held within the borders of Trilleah, Jennifer thought. But when she heard the words of Simeon, she realized she'd not thought nearly big enough thoughts about this dark and terrible land.

Oh, my dear one, she heard her Shailma say. *You have seen such a small part of this great and terrible land. Only one one-hundredth of the land have you walked or seen or experienced. The maps that you search and rely on show only the smallest portion of a land far too vast for you to imagine.*

Jennifer could hardly believe what she was hearing, but the voice was clearly that of her Shailma, for she had come to know it well.

Simeon's words were interrupted here and there with a sound that Jennifer recognized.

"Does anyone else hear that?" she asked. Nobody did. The land was silenced, and they had journeyed so far from the forest that even the usual groaning of the Waiting Ones could not reach their ears.

The sound, Jennifer knew, was waves crashing upon shores. Yes, it was undoubtedly a sea of some sort. As they walked, straightened up now and no longer hunching down, the sound became louder and louder and louder.

"I hear it," Sam said.

"Me too," whispered Bella.

"What is it?" Judah asked. "It sounds like water smashing into rocks." It reminded both the twins of the sound they used to fall asleep to when their parents would take them camping on the beaches by the ocean. They loved the sound then, but being young and loving the water and the beach, they had no idea how dangerous it could be. They never realized the power of the crashing waves until right now.

"That is exactly what it is, Judah," Jennifer said. "Don't you see it?" she asked. Nobody did. The mist was still too thick, and they were yet a ways off. But as they kept walking and listening, the sea came into view and shocked them into silence.

It was unbelievable. There were no words to describe the vastness of it. The crashing waves were deafening and the water was splashing up and drenching the Travelers. They failed to notice, though, because they were completely taken with what was laid out before them. No matter how hard they tried, the Travelers could not make their minds accept what their eyes were seeing.

"I had no idea!" Judah said.

"My eyes deceive me," Bella whispered. Her words were barely heard.

"In all the journeys, the maps have never shown such a thing," Pierce mumbled. He rubbed his head and seemed greatly puzzled and indeed, he was. They all were!

"None of that matters now, I suppose. Here we are … and here it is," Jennifer said firmly. "The question now is not where it came from but rather, what does it mean for us since the path led us right here, to the sea."

As they stood wide-eyed, getting more and more drenched by the crashing waves, they watched as all the mist they had been blindly walking through was being pulled toward the sea. It was like a vacuum had been turned on below the water and was sucking every fiber of the mist into itself.

The mist hovered now over the sea and was thick. The Travelers looked behind them and saw it was clear where they'd just been. They could see a long way behind them and hoped the army wouldn't be able to see them now that the mist no longer hid their whereabouts.

For a reason they didn't yet know, the mist had been pulled toward the sea to try and hide it. It could not, however, for the sea was considerably large and unable to be hidden.

"Pierce," Sam said inquisitively. "If the maps didn't show the sea, and we are standing at its shore now, where was the path drawn?"

It seemed like a reasonable question, but there was no reasonable answer. They were all equally puzzled. Finally, Bella was reminded by Shura of the other map—the one that had refused to be read. She spoke up.

"Hey, remember back in the caves, Pierce? You laid out two maps."

"Yes, of course, I remember," he snapped, which was unusual since it was Bella he was speaking to. "What of it?" he asked.

"Well, I was wondering if maybe that other map would have shown us this sea?" She didn't seem to notice how Pierce was talking to her, or maybe she decided to ignore it. Either way, Bella was as sweet as honey in her wonderings.

"Could be I 'spose," he replied, much kinder now. "I don't know how to read a map that refuses to be read, though. Any suggestions?" he asked the Travelers.

Nobody said anything for a while; they were pondering possible suggestions. Nobody came up with any, however, and Pierce was left to figure it out on his own.

"I don't know how to do it," he finally said. He did pull the stubborn map out of his pocket, however, but was careful not to let it get wet.

"Just lay it out, I guess," Jennifer muttered. She wasn't sure she wanted the idea to be heard, so she said it quietly. It was heard anyway, and it was not appreciated. It was, after all, a ridiculous suggestion.

"We can't just lay the map out," Pierce snapped.

"Why not?" Bella asked. "I see no caves or cover around here, do you?" They each turned their heads this way and that, searching for any possible covered place where they could try laying the map out again. There was none.

"There's a slight overhang on that rock," Matt pointed out. "It doesn't seem like much, but if that's all there is then that will have to do."

"I doubt it, Matt, I don't think it will do at all." Pierce handed Matt the map and Matt sheepishly put his hand out to take it. "If you think it'll do then be my guest. Give it a try," Pierce said. He was particularly foul right about now, and everyone was getting tired of it.

"Pierce," Bella said with her sweetest voice. "I think we're only trying to figure out a solution here."

"Yup," he replied in a slightly better—but not completely better—tone. Jennifer rolled her eyes dramatically when she saw that Judah had looked her way. He just winked back at her knowing how greatly Pierce annoyed his sister at the best of times. This was far from the best of times, though.

Matt took the map and moved toward the overhang of the rock. It was a small space but he was right, there were no other options. Some went with him, and some stayed where they were. Those who stayed where they were had no hope that the map would cooperate and those who went with Matt trusted that it would, for they needed it to.

Matt set the map down under the overhang and stepped back. Nothing happened. He picked it up and shook it so that it half-opened and set it back down. The map jumped and shook and folded right back into itself again.

"This is ridiculous," Matt said picking up the map again. "Let's try forcing it," he suggested. He took hold of two corners and Judah took hold of two corners. "Pull," Matt said. They pulled, and the map popped open.

"Yeah," Jennifer jumped up and down, but her excitement was premature, as the map was fighting against itself to show what it had to show. A few large boulders raised themselves up but then, before they were fully in view, the map shook itself—best it could, being pulled between the boys—and the boulders disappeared.

"Come on, you stupid map," Jennifer wailed. "We need your help!"

"Try pulling it tighter," Matt suggested. "Maybe if it can't shake itself, what is shown will stay shown." Judah pulled harder but the map put up a full-blown fight.

"Sam," Matt hollered. "Come help!" Sam ran over and took one of the corners.

"Pierce, we need you," Judah shouted.

Pierce went, but not quickly. He thought the idea was foolish, but if it was going to work at all, and if they were going to force the map to give up its information, he wanted to be a part of it. He grabbed one of the other corners and held on tight.

"Don't let it squirm," Judah hollered. The girls moved back to watch and see what was going to happen. They knew they needed the information the map was refusing to give up, and they held their breath in hopes that this would work.

It did! Eventually, when the map realized it could not hide its particulars any longer, it showed what the Travelers had been waiting to see. Not that they particularly wanted to see what the map was showing, but as they had learned so painfully in the past, knowing unwanted information was still far more helpful than not knowing it.

And so, they looked hard and stared silently in disbelief until finally, the boys let go of the map and watched as it crumpled itself into a ball and was swept into the sea.

Chapter 19

Dirty Souls

"Well, I hope we never need to look at that map again," Sam complained.

"We barely got to look at it this time," Judah added.

"I don't understand what it was showing … it sure didn't draw any path!" Matt grumbled. They were all quite annoyed with the map, but it made no difference now since it was gone.

They walked back to the shore and looked for a way around the sea. They looked this way and saw more of the sea. They looked that way and saw still more of the sea. There was no way around it and no way over it and they most certainly were not about to go through it.

"What are we going to do?" Jennifer cried. "We're so close to collecting all the tablets, but without these last ones, the others are useless!" She was getting herself worked up—again—and someone might have tried to calm her if everyone else was not equally as worked up and frustrated and agitated as she was.

The Travelers were busy looking for a way—any way—to the other side of the sea. They didn't even know for certain if there *was* another side to this sea, but they imagined there must be. Surely they had not journeyed clear to the other side of Trilleah already! And if they were not at the other side of the Dark Land, then that other side must be somewhere beyond this sea that was stretched out before them.

While they were busy looking ahead, they failed to notice what—or who—had snuck up behind. Miriam had been following close behind the Travelers the entire time. Since they left Asphelia's Hollow, she had been with them, even though they were unaware of her presence.

The Reptilian Mindbender had managed to stay back far enough to be unnoticed. When the army chased the Travelers into the hollow, Miriam was aware that on the other end of that hollow was a cave. She knew the Travelers would be coming out there, and while it took them much longer than she had hoped, they did eventually exit exactly where she expected them to.

She was waiting for them there, hidden. The Travelers were so busy looking for the army that they never even noticed Miriam hidden among the rocks. She was relieved they were preoccupied with the army since that was exactly the purpose of the army at the moment. It was a distraction which made it easy for her to tag along unnoticed—all the way to the sea. There was no going back for the Travelers, and the way forward seemed impassible. Now, here they stood. All the while, Miriam's eyes never left them.

"Stupid Travelers," she whispered. "I'll get those tablets. If it's the last thing I do in Shrailzhar's land, I promise you, I will get them."

"I think the map showed to go this way," Pierce said.

"To the east. It was hard to tell, but yes, I agree." Bella nodded toward the east as she confirmed the way with Pierce. "It looked like there was a path somewhere in this direction." She had no idea; she wasn't close enough to the map to see anything. It seemed like nobody else knew either, and as much as Pierce got under everyone's skin, Bella did trust him—mostly.

So, they began heading toward the eastern side of the sea. Bella caught up to Pierce and grabbed onto his arm to let him know she was beside him. He looked down at her and smiled. "We'll be OK you know," he said.

"I know," she replied.

"I want to ask you something, and I need you to be honest with me," Bella said firmly. Pierce stiffened up a bit, for he had much to hide.

"OK," he answered her.

"Well," Bella began. "That first Solstice journey that Miriam was with us, the one where I found her in the forest ..."

"Yes," Pierce interrupted, "I know the one."

"There have been a few things that have bothered me since that first time I saw her." Bella gave Pierce no time to respond and continued. "She seemed to know a lot about Trilleah and the land and things that a first-time Traveler would have no way of knowing."

"Is that what's been bothering you?" Pierce asked assuming she was done talking.

"No. Well, partly yes, but not only that," Bella stammered.

"Then what?" he asked. Pierce sounded patient with Bella, so she felt this was the right time to bring up what she'd overheard back in the hollow on that day.

"Well, Pierce, I heard you and her talking—arguing really—in that one passageway at the back of the Eating Chamber. I was in that passageway with you—only you didn't know it at the time."

"You were?" he asked. Bella wasn't sure whether his response meant that he was surprised she'd heard their conversation or confused about what she was talking about. Nevertheless, she continued.

"I heard Miriam say that if you'd have listened to her that neither of you would be in this mess ... or that she was only here because you refused to listen to her and stay away ... or something like that."

The handsome, dark-haired snarly Pierce looked down at her.

Yes, he's confused, she thought. But about what precisely, she didn't know.

"I'm sorry, Bella, but I don't remember what you're talking about," he replied. She knew he did, though, because the look on his face said he was surprised that someone heard Miriam's comment or any of their argument that day. The fact was that Pierce knew exactly

Page 178

what Bella was talking about because it had bothered him as well for quite a long time.

"She sounded angry with you, Pierce. You were definitely angry with her. How did you and Miriam know each other before Trilleah?" Bella asked. "And be honest because we both know that Miriam is not one of us—she's not a Traveler or a Curse Breaker. I'm afraid she could cause much delay to us ever breaking the curse; maybe stop us altogether …"

He listened quietly while they continued walking east, wondering if everyone else had heard the argument between him and Miriam so long ago. The others seemed to be chatting among themselves, so Pierce opened his mouth to tell Bella a story—a story she wouldn't want to hear—a story he had buried for a long time, wanting to avoid the day when he'd have to tell it.

"Truth is a funny thing, Bella," he began. "When we think we want to know something and then find that thing out, well, once we know it, we might learn that we didn't really want to know it in the first place. You can never un-know it. You can never go back."

She never liked it much when Pierce talked in riddles. She was much more of a straightforward person and didn't like how he danced around topics like he was doing now.

"Pierce, how do you know Miriam?" she repeated her question with much more firmness.

"Well … Miriam is … Miriam … is my cousin."

"What?" Bella shrieked. "Why have you never mentioned this?" Bella demanded to know. "Pierce, that is necessary information to share, don't you think?"

"No," he replied. "I don't think it matters at all. If I had thought it did, I'd have told you."

"Why were you arguing then?" she asked. Bella had only two cousins, and they never argued with one another. They were very close, but then again, not everyone was like her, she supposed.

Do not let him change the subject, Bella heard from Shura. *He will not want to answer your questions about the girl, so keep asking until he does. The information is of utmost importance to the last of your journeys in Trilleah.*

Bella was not one to hear her Shailma just any old time. So, because she was so clearly hearing Shura now, it made her keenly aware of just how important finding out this information was.

"Pierce, why were you arguing?" she asked for the third time.

"You won't understand, but since you're not going to drop it, here it is. When Peter ran into the street—and his soul was stolen by the Trows—Miriam was there."

Now it was Bella who looked confused. He'd never mentioned any of this before, and she wondered why.

Why keep it a secret, she wondered. She didn't have to wonder long.

"Miriam saw the whole thing. She saw me throw the ball because she was playing with us; she blamed me. That little wretch said I did it on purpose."

"She was the one who ran in and told my mom what had happened. She said I was jealous of Peter and that I pushed him into the street." His voice rose as he finished the sentence. "She lied to my mother and said I pushed him. But Bella, I never did such a thing. You have to believe me!

"I didn't push Peter… and I was never jealous of him."

Pierce looked as though he might begin to cry, so Bella touched his arm to calm him.

"I believe you, Pierce. But why were you arguing with her in the hollow?" she asked the question for a fourth time now.

"Back there, in the hollow …" his voice trailed off as his memories carried him back to that place. "Miriam followed me here," he finally said. "I told her not to come, and I was angry with her because she told my mother those things and my mother believed her. Mother's been angry with me ever since."

"I was just a little boy, but my mom believed the horrible lies Miriam had told her. Maybe Peter *was* her favorite; I don't know! But at that moment, my mom said some horrible things to me and said she had always preferred Peter. I thought she was just upset, but Miriam continued to remind me over and over that my mother probably wished it was me that had gotten hit by the car, instead of Peter."

He stopped talking and rubbed his face. Bella knew he wanted to say more, so she walked along quietly, waiting. She didn't wait long.

"I told Miriam not to come to Trilleah because I never wanted to see her again. After I had come to the Dark Land a couple of times— you were here, Bella, remember? I told her about Trilleah. I shouldn't have. I should never have told her, but I did. From then on she wanted to come. She kept bragging and making promises that she could break the curse by herself."

"That little wretch was always looking for more attention, more power, more influence over people." As he was telling the story, he seemed to be getting more and more upset. Bella was about to find out why and she listened carefully.

"I didn't want her to come because only those with a pure heart can come to Trilleah and survive!" Pierce explained. "Did you know that, Bella?" he asked.

"No," she mumbled. He had been right, though. None of this made sense to Bella, but still, having the information helped even if was confusing.

"So Miriam did not have a pure heart?" she asked, still working on understanding.

"Oh no, Bella, not at all," he snapped. "You see, you and the twins came to Trilleah to free the souls of the Waiting Ones."

Well yes, she thought. *Of course, we did.*

"And Sam came to free his sister and Matt came to free his father and so on. I came," he continued in a quieter voice now, "to help free Peter. Sometimes I think I have a pure heart, but other times, I wonder if I want to free the soul of Peter so my mother would know that I didn't push him in front of that car like Miriam told her."

"Oh, Pierce," Bella sighed. "Of course, you didn't push him."

"Sometimes I wonder, though," he said again, but she refused to believe it since Bella had grown fond of the young man and she'd seen into his heart many times. She knew he had a pure heart even if he questioned it himself. The way he would talk about Peter, Bella never doubted that he loved his brother very much; enough to trade places with him if such a thing were possible—which of course, it wasn't.

Bella was trying to think of something to say that would bring peace to her friend, but before she could come up with anything helpful, Pierce spoke again.

"Anyhow," he said, "none of that makes any difference now because Miriam did not come with a pure heart. She came with an evil heart and evil intentions … now Trilleah has stolen her soul but in a whole different way than the Trows took Peter's.

"What are you talking about?" she asked. "How?"

The others had gathered around by now since Pierce and Bella had slowed down. They overheard much of what Pierce had said already and waited impatiently to hear more. The Travelers had not said anything up until this time—only listened. But now, they each moved closer and listened a little harder; they wanted to know how Trilleah had stolen Miriam's soul and if it could steal their souls too.

"Well, I suppose her soul has not been *stolen* exactly. But her heart has been turned to black, and she has become a part of the king's army."

"How?" Matt asked, clearly flabbergasted.

Pierce took a deep breath and began to explain things that not even he understood.

"She came to Trilleah with an impure heart and with impure motives, so the king was able to persuade her with his lies and promises of many things. Miriam only came to Trilleah to try and stop me from freeing the souls because she had lied and didn't want that lie to be found out. She followed me and told many more lies after that to cover up the first lies. She has told so many lies that I'm convinced she doesn't know what the truth is anymore.

"Because of all that, King Shrailzhar was able to convince Miriam that there was a way to stop me—to stop any of us from freeing the souls—and she told that wretched king that she'd do anything to keep the souls under the curse. Peter's specifically, but if it meant she had to keep every soul locked away, it made no never mind to her."

As Pierce continued his explaining, it was beginning to make a wee bit of sense. But really, not very much at all. "The king made Miriam a Reptilian Mindbender," he whispered.

"WHAT is a Reptilian Mindbender?" Sam wanted to know.

"Why, Sam," Pierce said flatly, "it's one who bends minds this way and that—or whichever way she wants it to go! The Dark Deceivers have taken over her soul and given her many powers. She's only still in her body to hide her true identity from us … for now."

Chapter 20

Telling Secrets

Now Pierce had everyone's full attention. They were still walking but at a snail's pace. Everyone was concerned with this new information they were just now finding out about Miriam—especially Matt and Jennifer, who'd been personally afflicted by Miriam's cursing ability.

"But … where did those powers come from?" Matt asked.

Pierce thought he would never have to share such secrets; after all, Miriam was his cousin. However, the time seemed to be right for revealing such things and besides that, his Shailma was leading him and giving him the courage to speak the unspeakable.

He knew that Miriam could very well curse his own lips, but she was back in the hollow—as far as he knew—so she may not realize that he was revealing her secrets just yet.

"The first time you saw Miriam in the forest, Bella, it was not her first time in Trilleah. She had followed me one other time."

Bella wasn't surprised. It explained how Miriam had known so much about the Dark Land. At least one thing finally made some sense.

"Mhm," was all she said, though, because she wanted Pierce to keep going, both with his feet and with his story.

"The first time she was here, the Army of Trilleah caught her and dragged her before the king. Now, as I see you are all horrified at such a thought and want to blame her horridness on that, just wait." Pierce stopped walking for a minute, and everyone stopped with him.

"What is it?" Judah asked.

"I don't know which way to go," Pierce replied. The Travelers looked ahead and saw that any possibility of a path had been reduced to almost nothing. The sea was laid out to their left, and their right, thick overgrown brush covered the ground leaving them nowhere to walk.

"Oh dear," Bella said as was her usual comment when things became frustrating.

"Can we sit for a minute and have lunch?" Jennifer asked. After all, she had left Westlock long before the others and hadn't eaten a thing since the few kernels of popcorn she'd tried to munch on last night. With her tongue outrageously swollen and painful, even the popcorn she did manage to eat was only a very small amount.

"Good idea, J," Bella said. "There's a tiny inlet there, in the brush." Nobody else said anything, but all headed to where Bella had pointed, and sat down. She opened her cloak and began pulling out a container of this and a bag of that. She handed it all to Judah, who set everything on the ground.

As they grabbed handfuls of nuts and a sandwich or two, Judah spoke up.

"Pierce, continue please!" he said. Pierce needed no more coaxing. Now that the story had been started, it needed to be told all the way to the end.

"Bella, do you remember the first time you had Jennifer come to Trilleah?" he asked. It seemed like he was changing the subject and nobody wanted that.

"Of course," Bella replied.

"And do you recall that you were annoyed with me because I had disappeared for a while?"

"Yes," she said, realizing where his story was heading.

"Well, I hadn't simply disappeared as you'd thought," he said. "I went to help Miriam, but I couldn't help her because she didn't want to be helped."

"What?" one said, bewildered.

"Why not?" another asked, confused.

Pierce said nothing for a moment because he took a minute to munch down one sandwich and then another. When the last bite was swallowed, he continued. "I found where the king had taken her and thought it was odd that it was so easy to track them. I figured the king was a complete imbecile because it was so easy.

"But then, when I was taking cover in the bush and listening, I realized that he hadn't been concerned about hiding Miriam. He didn't take her far because he wanted her to be able to return quickly. What the king had done was offer Miriam a deal," he said.

"What do you mean, 'a deal?' " Matt asked, confused. They were all confused. This entire explanation was confusing.

"I mean," Pierce continued, "that the king told Miriam she could have great power—power to change someone's thoughts or put a curse on their tongues or even their flesh, but not on their souls, for that was the Trows' right and theirs alone."

The eyes of the Travelers grew large as they could hardly believe what they were hearing. It sounded like a story far too outrageous to be true. Matt and Jennifer knew perfectly that Miriam had done something to them, and so no matter how far-fetched the story sounded, it was indeed a true one.

"Just like that?" Judah asked. "He just gave her these mind powers and whatnot?"

"Not exactly," Pierce said. "There's more. The king had said he noticed Miriam was very good at lying and that she had no sadness or remorse about it. She agreed, almost as if she was proud of such things."

"It's like a game to me," she told the king. "And I always win that game." Pierce shook his head. It disgusted him.

"I hated hearing her say that to the king, especially after the lie she'd told to my mom … but it was the truth, I suppose." He paused a minute and it was clear that the effects of Miriam's lie to his mom were very difficult for him to talk about.

"The king told her that since she was so good at it, and because she liked the power it gave her, that he could give her far more power if she would make an exchange with him."

"What was the exchange?" Sam asked. "I'm not sure I want to know. I know it's not a good one, but I understand many more things now, after hearing about this."

Pierce swigged a few mouthfuls of Roota Juice before continuing. "The king said he would touch Miriam's mouth and give power to her tongue to make believable any lie she decided to tell and along with it, give her the power to place a curse on the tongues of others who tried to tattle on her."

One quiver after another ran up Jennifer's spine as she listened to the deal. She knew that was how Miriam's tongue became forked— the lying tongue of a serpent—and why she was able to do the things to Jennifer's mind that she'd done in the Labyrinth. She knew that was how Miriam was able to curse her tongue, and why it burned when Miriam had touched it.

"So it was the lying tongue then that made the king know he could get Miriam to help him?" Jennifer asked.

"Exactly, J," Pierce said. Now, he had never called her "J" before. He had never called her anything before except for unkind things. She was not sure if she liked it or not, but thinking about Miriam and her deal with the king, what Pierce decided to call her right now didn't matter one bit.

Pierce continued. "It was her lies that caught the attention of King Shrailzhar and opened the door for him to come in and trap Miriam."

"She was tricked, I think," Jennifer said. Part of her wanted to feel sorry for the girl, and nearly did. But there was no way Jennifer was going to be tricked as well, so she refused to let herself feel one shred of sadness for such a wretch as Miriam.

But Pierce did feel sorry for the girl; very sorry indeed. While he blamed himself for the Trows stealing Peter's soul, he also felt responsible for the state Miriam found herself in. He was angry with her, of course, but not so angry that he didn't feel deeply saddened. What she didn't realize was that the little measure of power she'd been given for a short amount of time was going to cost her soul; a price far too high to pay for any amount of power.

If the Travelers *did* manage to find the couple remaining clay tablets, and if they *were* somehow able to figure out the writing on them and break the curse and release the souls of the ones they were here for, Miriam would never be free. Her soul belonged to the king. He had bought her and she belonged to him.

While the hundreds of thousands of souls that were trapped in the forest had been stolen, Miriam's soul had been given willingly; it would never find release. For all eternity, she would belong to the king.

After Pierce had explained all that he knew, all that he had thought, and all that he could think of to explain, he was quiet. He had nothing left to say. He was completely spent.

They all sat quietly, considering and pondering all these things they'd just heard; unbelievable things. Among them was Kaija Mae, who had far greater power over Miriam than Miriam had over her, although none of the Travelers knew anything of that. She knew far more information about Miriam, and the deal between her and the king than even Pierce knew, because Kaija Mae had been in Trilleah since the very first tree held the very first soul.

She said nothing now, though, for now was not the time. But there would be a time, and it would come quickly. All these things were going to come quickly since time was running out. Kaija Mae would be ready when the time came. She looked at Aviel and winked at him. He read every silent word that her wink whispered and he returned it with just as much detail.

Aviel, Kaija Mae, and all the others who'd been here since the beginning had a great deal more knowledge and understanding of the things of Trilleah—and all those in it. They waited patiently for the time to come when they could finally come forward with all they knew.

The one thing that none of them knew, however, was that the king had given Miriam an even greater assignment; one that she thought would be as easy as could be, and she was working furiously on carrying it out. Even now, this assignment was the reason she was lurking in dark corners and under bits of fallen sky.

Miriam had no idea, however, when she accepted such an assignment, that Jennifer would give her so much trouble. She never considered there would be one among them who was so trusting of her Shailma and so obedient to his leading that it would be nearly impossible to defeat her. Miriam was confident, however, that it was only a matter of time before little Jennifer gave up and Miriam would have the victory.

"It's simple," the king had told Miriam on her second trip to his Dark Land. "All you must do is destroy the clay tablets!" He said it as if it was the easiest thing in the world. By her second trip, however, Miriam had become confident in the king's reliance on her, so she made a demand of her own.

"And if I do?" she asked. "What's in it for me?"

King Shrailzhar didn't enjoy sharing his power—or his throne—but Miriam had become a valuable and necessary tool for his success in owning all the souls on the earth. He needed her, and they both knew it. So he asked, "What is it, Miriam, that you want in trade?"

"It's simple," she said to the horrible king. "I want a throne of my own and to be the Princess of the Dark Land for all eternity."

She expected the king to say no, or to offer something less than what she'd requested, but to her great surprise he agreed and had a covenant written up straightaway. Then, the king's actions disgusted even Miriam. Nevertheless, she pushed those feelings down, lying now to herself, and did what he commanded.

"Hold out your hand," the king said. When she did, he took his own hand and placed it beside hers. He shouted an order to the general of his army who was nearby. The general pulled out a razor-sharp dagger, deeply slicing the backs of their hands.

The king winced and shook his hand. He took his finger and wiped it across the gushing cut on Miriam's hand. Then he signed just above his name on the covenant in her blood and commanded Miriam to do the same.   She did. Each signed their name in the blood of the other, making the covenant eternally unbreakable.

Miriam headed to the hollow to grant the king his request and hold up her end of the agreement.

"I WILL destroy the tablets," Miriam told the king. "Get my throne ready."

Shrailzhar nodded toward the girl, who had wrapped a cloth around her hand to stop the bleeding.

You should have read the fine print, you stupid wretch, the king thought to himself. *You should always read the fine print.*

Under the Sea

The Travelers would find out about Miriam's blood-signed covenant soon enough since the girl was moving in close now. She had hoped to steal the tablets from the hollow without anyone seeing her. However, it was clear that was no longer going to be an option since Matt had brought the clay tablets with him.

Bella had a feeling the tablets were no longer safe in Asphelia's Hollow, so she had given them to Matt—who had hidden them in his cloak. She kept checking with him to make sure he still held them close fearing something terrible happening to the pieces of clay.

Miriam had held those cold, hard, brick-like tablets in her hands often, turning them around and running her fingers along the words scribbled on them. Every time she had a chance—without the Travelers around to bother her, or question her, or become suspicious—she would lay the tablets out and count them.

She'd gotten excited as she counted them the last time. One by one she laid them on the eating stump as she counted; four … five … six … seven …

Every time her fingers touched the cold clay, she wanted to destroy them but that was not the best way to do it. Oh no … She must be patient and wait for ALL the tablets to be collected and then destroy them all at once. If she became too anxious and destroyed only some, the Travelers would know her identity and probably destroy her! Miriam knew she had to be patient just a little while longer, but her anticipation was getting the best of her.

There was only one way to do such a task … so she waited. Oh, how she plotted and schemed about exactly how she would do it. But since the Travelers had come all this way and had only a couple left to find, she thought maybe she'd been patient long enough.

"After all, two have already been broken today, but not destroyed." She knew they had to be destroyed completely—beyond repair or recognition.

"I will throw them into the sea," she thought as she watched the Travelers eat their lunch. Miriam grabbed her belly as it began to rumble. She was so close to the Travelers now that she had to be careful not to let them discover her. "I cannot believe how slow they are being," she whispered to the wind. "Hurry up … HURRY UP."

Of course, there was no one around to hear her, but she didn't care because she didn't need anyone else's help. She knew that the army would help if she asked, but Miriam was selfish and not willing to share her throne with anyone, so she determined to do this herself.

The army had already proven to be a great distraction earlier today and she knew if she did need them, she could call on them and they'd come running. Miriam tried not to call on the army, though. They had very little control over themselves and she didn't want the Travelers dead—only gone. She wanted them to be far, far away from the land of which she would soon be the Princess.

Soon all this will belong to me, she thought, glancing around the Dark Land. *I need to move fast before that idiot king destroys it on me.*

You see, Miriam had a plan all her own. She would secure her place in the kingdom, earn her throne, and turn the Army of Shrailzhar so that they were on her side. Then, when the king learned to trust her, Miriam would send the army against him. It would be simple because even the king's own army hated him. Once dead, she would own it all. Oh, the plans she had for this land. First, the name would be changed, for she deeply hated the name Trilleah.

Slow yourself down, Miriam, she thought. *You get ahead of yourself sometimes. But not this time; this time I will succeed.*

Miriam got so wound up in her plans and thoughts and devilish dreams for the land that she barely noticed as the Travelers packed up the last bites of their lunch and were ready to move on.

All the while that they had sat semi-hidden in the covering of shrubs and trees discussing Miriam and learning of her deepest secrets, they had also been searching for a path to take. It took longer than they had hoped, but Matt eventually spotted a little trail just inside the overgrown, bushy hedges.

"It's probably better there," he said when the others finally agreed that it really was a trail. "We might be hidden a while longer, rather than being right out in the open here along the sea."

"I still cannot believe there is a sea there," Judah said. "My eyes are seeing it, but my brain can't believe it." They each nodded and agreed at just how outrageous it all was. Quickly, they moved ahead until they were in a single line and wandering down the trail to somewhere they did not know. They tried to stay hidden; they had no idea the one they needed to stay hidden from had been watching them the whole time.

The land was beginning to blow a lot more now, with a storm of leaves swirling both in the air and on the ground. Within minutes, the narrow trail they were on was covered completely, and it seemed the land did not want their feet on its path.

"We're going to have to go back out along the shore," Pierce said. "There's no other way."

Sam started to argue but realized that arguing with Pierce was a waste of time; he was probably right anyway. There was no other way.

Sometimes, no matter how badly one wants another way, there just isn't one to be had.

"Maybe if we get far enough down the shoreline there will be a bridge," someone suggested.

"A bridge to where?" someone else wanted to know. Nobody gave an answer because really, there was no answer to give. There was no bridge, and the shore went on forever.

"I know the gates are broken down so we can't get trapped in Trilleah," Judah said. "Does that mean we don't have to leave the land?" His wondering got everyone else wondering. "Can we stay inside the gates and find the remaining tablets?"

"That would make sense," Jennifer said, "although I don't want to stay!" Nobody did—especially since the sun was setting and the wind that had picked up a while back was now beginning to swirl and stir up the sea like a ravenous brute. The waves had become outrageously large. Just as one would rise to its peak and smash down, sending currents of smelly water to cover the Travelers, another would begin to rise. One after another after another, the waves grew larger both in size and number.

There seemed no end to this sea and its waves. The Travelers had stopped without realizing it, mesmerized by the smashing waves and swirling waters. Some wanted to keep going, others wanted to turn back.

"There's no use," Sam complained. "We're getting nowhere. We are just going around and around and around!"

"Sam, we are not going around and around; the sea is," Matt said. He moved toward Sam to try and comfort the boy. Even though

Sam had grown to be very tall, towering above everyone else, he was still just a kid, and Matt felt bad for him.

"I can't do it," Sam howled. "I can't!"

The Travelers hovered around Sam and tried to console him. Kaija Mae moved closer and tried to bring some encouragement, but nothing was working. Even her quiet singing—which was usually a source of great comfort—was empty for the poor boy. He was simply overwhelmed, and it seemed too much for the young lad.

With everyone huddled around him, it took them all by surprise when Sam suddenly screamed with his whole voice.

"LOOK!" he wailed and pointed over their heads toward the sea. Everyone did look.

They searched his face to see where he was looking and then turned to find what he was looking at. They didn't have to search long. As they turned their faces toward the sea, they could not help but find what had caused Sam to shout and point.

Even though the mist was putting forth its best efforts to hide all that lay in the sea—for the sea held a great many unimaginable beasts and devilish creatures and cursed secrets—it could no longer hide the one thing that Sam had spotted.

Rising slowly from the deep of the sea just a short ways from the shore was the most gigantic and gruesome sea creature any one of them had ever seen. Now, none of them had ever seen any sea monsters before this one, but Judah did recall seeing something similarly gruesome in a movie once.

"I wasn't supposed to watch it, but I did anyway," he said. "I had nightmares for months. The savage in that movie looked an awful lot … like … like this thing here."

It was more of a sea demon, really. The higher it rose from the deep of the sea, the more hideous it became. It lifted part of itself higher and higher and higher, while part of it remained beneath the water.

The mist rose up around it, trying to hide the demon sea creature, but it was unable to. It was just too big. The mist hovered thick but could not cover it. The winds were of no help either. The mists had to fight hard against it, but they refused to be blown away.

The Travelers were hunched down, balancing on the backs of their feet and hiding inside of their cloaks. They were whispering so quietly that anyone who spoke was not sure their words went much farther than the inside of their own hoods.

"I've heard of things like this," Matt whispered. "In our history class recently we talked about something an awful lot like this, but the books said nobody had ever actually seen one. It was called a Leviathan, but it was thought to be a myth!" Matt went on to describe the beast they had studied in his class, and as the water demon got closer and rose up out of the water higher, they could see that it was, indeed, exactly what Matt had described.

"The Leviathan," Jennifer whispered.

"The Leviathan," they all repeated.

Nobody moved; not even Miriam. While she knew the Leviathan was kept beneath the deepest parts of the dark sea, she'd never seen it nor had she wanted to. Now that it was stretching itself up in front of her, she realized how greatly she had underestimated the great water demon.

There wasn't much that frightened Miriam about Trilleah. After all, she knew the king. But she also knew the Leviathan was the one creature that had rebelled against the king, and Shrailzhar had lost all control of it. The Leviathan had no need to obey the king; the king was afraid of him.

"Who can subdue ME? Who dares to harness ME?" the great water demon had shrieked at the king.

"If you can put a bridle my mouth," the Leviathan had challenged Shrailzhar, "I will submit to you and be at your command for all eternity. However," he roared, "if you fail, I shall snuff out your life, and you will become nothing more than a mist, added to my great cloud of mists that is indeed, the remains of all those who came before you and tried to rule me."

Of course, the king refused even to try such an unmanageable feat as bridling the Leviathan. He was smarter than most dull-minded beings and so decided he would rather leave the Leviathan to rule the sea and harness the mists than to become part of the mists himself.

"After all," King Shrailzhar had reasoned to his army, "Trilleah is enormous in size, so if that unruly Leviathan wants to have the sea for himself, so be it. I will rule the rest of the land and stay away from the sea altogether!"

The Travelers were without knowledge of any such information, however, and now hunching in the brush and trying to stay hidden—and alive—had become their one and only goal.

That goal was becoming easier and easier because the sun had begun its descent and the sky was growing dim. However, the Travelers had still not found the clay tablet and every path they could find kept leading them straight to the sea.

With all the Travelers looking forward, straining their eyes to watch the Leviathan, none of them were looking anywhere else. If they had been, they'd have noticed that Miriam had snuck up close and was nearly right beside Matt.

It would be difficult to notice her now, though. None had seen her join them and with everyone hidden deep inside their cloaks, they all looked eerily the same. Who could tell one from another?

This was Miriam's plan the whole time, and she was giddy to see how easily it had worked. The Travelers were so distracted by the Leviathan and the mists that were still trying to cover the creature, that Miriam was able to walk right up and blend into the cloaked group.

"Oh, you stupid, simple-minded Travelers," she seethed inside her hood. "How easy you are to fool. Those tablets will be in my hands shortly and when they are, oh great Leviathan, you shall be my puppet as I throw them all into your sea. You will owe me, and I will collect full payment."

Wolves Among Us

Leviathan threw his head back and let out a howl like had never been heard before; neither in this land nor any other. He was angry. It was rare his mists became so stirred up, but they were stirred up now and they were ferocious.

The whole sky above the sea was moving; shifting like sand being shaken through a sieve. The mists were becoming violent, it appeared, and small funnel-looking shapes were beginning to form. The Travelers watched in horror as these small tornados sucked in pieces of the mists and spat them out again. Over and over again, sucking in and spitting out. Leviathan was agitated—never a good way for a Leviathan to be.

The Travelers could not look away; their attention was completely captured by the happenings above the sea.

When the towering water demon threw his head back, the Travelers could see that right below his jaw, was a hook. It most assuredly was not supposed to be there, and it suddenly became clear that they were not the first ones to come upon this creature.

The hook looked like it had been there for a long time and had, over that time, grown right into his jaw. The hook was far bigger than any one of the Travelers—even Sam—and they wondered who would be able to throw a hook of such size. Besides that wondering, they wondered what happened to the ones who had thrown the hook. They wondered how big of a man it would take to throw a hook so large and where that man might be now, if, in fact, it was a man at all.

They would never know, however, and it made no difference one way or the other. Leviathan was about to make them forget they had even seen the hook … or the mists … or the sea.

Leviathan's neck had to be at least thirty feet long and there was a spiral of something shiny and jagged going all the way around it. The first section of whatever those jagged pieces were protruded from just above the sea. The Travelers had no idea how much of the demon monster was still hidden beneath the sea but decided it must be a great amount.

That first shiny piece looked about twelve inches across and ten inches high. The next one was slightly smaller and up just a few inches. From there, things that looked like broken pieces of mirror—since they were jagged, razor-sharp, and shone with the reflection of the sea—moved up Leviathan's neck; not straight up the back of the beast, like one might imagine, but in more of a spiral formation. They wrapped around his neck like an old spiral staircase with the last of them coming from the top of his head. It was not a horn, but more like a dagger of death.

As Leviathan whipped his head around sending out a sound that sent pain through the Travelers' ears and caused their blood to nearly freeze, whatever it was that protruded from the top of his ghastly head sliced through the mists. This way and that. It caused the mists to scurry away, but they came straight back as though lassoed by the wind.

As the Travelers watched such horror, trembling, and with their ears covered, it seemed the mists were telling a story of sorts. It became clear that the purpose of the mists was to cover the demon beast; to hide him. The Leviathan seemed not to want to be hidden.

The mists wanted to flee—that much was clear—yet they seemed completely unable to do so! It was mesmerizing and even though the Travelers wanted to look away, they couldn't force their eyes from the sight. Deciding whether the mists were trying to hide the Leviathan, or to move away from the beast, was impossible to tell for sure. It was like watching a dance where neither partner wanted to participate yet neither could walk away. The Travelers eventually gave up wondering about such things and turned their attention back to the hook in its jaw.

Miriam, however, was neither mesmerized by the mists nor concerned about the hook, for her own ambitions were far too exciting. Her heart was pounding and her palms were sweating. She had spent all her time today sliding one foot a few inches and then the other until she'd finally wiggled her way right into the middle of the Travelers. She was very satisfied with herself. The Travelers hunched closely together, so getting into the middle of them was tricky and time-consuming. Nevertheless, she'd done it, and she was ecstatic.

The good thing for Miriam was that she was a Mindbender and also that it was now quite dim in the land. When she'd felt one of the Travelers becoming annoyed with this one who was crowding them, she would throw other thoughts into their minds causing them to squeeze over and let her move right in.

Idiots! she laughed to herself. Their preoccupation with Leviathan had so distracted them that every shred of their attention was averted and their cautions of Miriam had been disarmed. *This is far too easy*, she thought. It was so easy, in fact, that Miriam was disappointed she was not given more opportunities to bend the minds of these simpletons.

Finally in a good position, she began her search for the one who was carrying the clay tablets.

"Matt?" she whispered into the hood of the nearest cloak, disguising her voice just enough to not raise suspicion.

"I'm Sam," was the reply. She moved more to the right.

"Matt?" she whispered again. Time after time she had the wrong cloak-covered Traveler until finally, the word she had been longing to hear reached her ears. It sounded like sweet music.

"What?" was the reply. She'd found him—that one who was between her and the tablets. Miriam knew there was still a couple uncollected and she needed to destroy all twelve, but she was becoming impatient.

"Besides," she reasoned with herself earlier in the hollow, "these might be enough."

As she wondered and plotted and reasoned, knowing perfectly well that the ones Matt carried would certainly *not* be enough, she came up with a plan.

"Perfect!" she had shouted in the hollow where the plan had been forged. She laughed as her excitement bounced off the rock walls and echoed back to her. "Perfect … perfect … perfect … perfect," came back to her time and time again.

So the plan was made.

Miriam would follow the Travelers, and when darkness fell over the land, she'd sneak in among them like a wolf among the dumbest of sheep. Of course, she would blend in perfectly because of the cloaks. Once she found Matt, she would persuade him to let her carry the tablets. They were heavy, after all—like bricks—and carrying so many of them for so long would have been wearing on him by this time; she was sure of it.

Then, as they found the next tablet, it would, of course, be handed directly to her and then all of them—the whole basket of them

—would be thrown into the sea. Her perfect plan was to then furiously enrage the Leviathan and cause him to flail about and crush the tablets into dust.

By the time those idiot Travelers figure out what I'm doing, it will be too late! The curse will be secure for all of eternity, and once stupid King Shrailzhar puts his trust in his royal princess—and indeed he will—the souls will belong to me. She would rule and reign the kingdom for all time. Thus, her plan was set, and it was perfect.

"What a beautifully excellent plan, my dear," she had said to herself back in the hollow.

"Why, thank you, Princess Miriam," she answered herself.

Miriam was indeed a wicked girl, but she had become much more wicked with every taste of power she received from King Shrailzhar. It seemed that power was what she was after; it fed her. The more she tasted of it, the more she wanted to have for herself.

So far so good, she thought. Her plan was coming together perfectly.

Now to persuade Matt to let her carry the tablets. This would be, by far, the most difficult piece of her entire plan because Matt was a true gentleman. He would never willingly let one of the girls carry something so heavy. Now that she'd found him, she disguised her voice. Deceiving him would be the only way.

"Matt," she whispered, for it's much easier to disguise one's voice if it's dipped in a whisper. "I can carry the tablets for a while; you must be getting tired. They are heavy!"

"I'm fine," he said. Matt wrongly mistook Miriam for Kaija Mae. "Did you forget the cloaks have pockets that hold the weight?"

He chuckled at such a thing. "I don't feel their weight at all," he whispered back.

Drat! Miriam thought. She had forgotten about that. She had rarely been trusted enough to carry anything in her cloak, so she'd never experienced their weight-bearing pockets.

I'm going to have to convince him, she decided. It only took her a minute to come up with something she was sure would work.

"I didn't mean the weight of the tablets," she whispered. "I meant the weight of the responsibility of carrying them. Certainly, you must feel it by now—especially with the sea laid out and the Leviathan breathing down on us ..."

She was sure this would work, this mental manipulation, but it would take a few minutes. She was willing to wait and went to work using her mind-bending powers to shape Matt's thoughts to match her own. Sooner than she expected, he answered her.

"Ya, I guess it is," he answered. "I hadn't thought about it until now."

Just to make sure she'd get her hands on those tablets, Miriam firmly touched Matt's arm. She had to gain his trust and make him think she was Kaija Mae. She knew that Matt would never let Jennifer carry the tablets because she was such a tiny girl, and much to Miriam's hateful bitterness, everyone protected Jennifer. Matt had an outrageous crush on Bella, so he would likely not let her carry the weight of such a burden either.

Yes, she would have to convince Matt that she was Kaija Mae.

The one thing that distinguished Kaija Mae from the other girls in Trilleah was her singing. That would be the key—that would be how Miriam would trick Matt into believing that he was talking to Kaija Mae. She would sing.

Very softly—for Miriam was not a good singer like Kaija Mae—she began singing. She pulled her hood forward to muffle her voice. She hoped that for Matt, it would only take the *idea* that any singing must belong to Kaija Mae. She was right.

"I suppose you're right, Kaija Mae," Matt finally whispered. Even while he said the words, something in his belly became unsettled. The singing continued for a little bit longer, but something seemed off. It didn't feel right.

Usually—always in fact—when Kaija Mae would begin singing, a stillness would fill the air. A depth of peace that was rarely felt would suddenly be felt by everyone as the words would come floating from Kaija Mae's lips and take up space in the air.

There was no peace riding on the wings of this song. It made Matt a little uncertain and he decided to hold the tablets ... at least for now.

Chapter 23

One Precarious Predicament

"Thanks, but I'm good with holding onto the tablets," Matt said. "I nearly forgot I was carrying them, so I guess they aren't causing me much turmoil." He pulled his hand inside the cloak and felt around until his fingers found the tablets. It was a rather important assignment Bella had asked of him, although he hadn't considered it as such until now—until it had been pointed out to him.

Rats, Miriam said under her breath but loud enough for Matt to hear. The voice didn't sound like Kaija Mae, but it wasn't loud enough for him to know for sure.

"Pardon?" he asked. Matt was beginning to feel that something was wrong here and he decided to be cautious; very cautious.

Mishan. He searched his mind for his Shailma since he had suddenly become aware that he needed direction and possibly even protection. From what, he didn't know … yet.

"Oh, nothing," Miriam whispered, but she could tell that Matt had become suspicious. She was foolish to try and copy Kaija Mae's singing. She knew—but had forgotten—that there was something in the girl's songs that couldn't be duplicated. She had also forgotten—or maybe she never realized in the first place—that the words in Kaija Mae's songs were not in any understandable language. Miriam had mistakingly sung in English.

Mishan, what's going on? Something's not right—something besides the Leviathan, that is. Matt could see that the Leviathan was going to be a problem, so it was not that which he was seeking his Shailma for; not yet.

You're right, Matt, Mishan whispered. *That is not the one you think it is. She is an impostor and she is after the tablets. You were wise not to hand them over. She will not give up easily. Be prepared for a battle.*

Now Matt's stomach felt sick. What would have happened if he'd have handed the tablets over? Who is this one trying to impersonate Kaija Mae? No wonder her songs didn't carry the same peace they normally held.

Matt didn't know what to do. He wanted to whisper to the others that there was an impostor among them—give them a hushed warning somehow. But that seemed impossible, with this one—this impostor—still holding onto his arm.

So, at what he thought was the instruction of Mishan, Matt suddenly stood up in the center of the cloaked Travelers and shouted.

"THERE IS AN IMPOSTER AMONG US!"

He expected that when he made her presence known to the others, the one beside him would let go of his arm and flee. That did not happen. Instead, she squeezed her fingers hard into his flesh and caused a sharp pain to shoot through his arm and up into his shoulder.

Instantly, he knew who this intruder was and warned the others.

"IT'S MIRIAM!" he shrieked as the pain became unbearable. The color left his skin, and he began to sweat.

He pulled her hand away from his arm and ripped his cloak off as well, for it had suddenly heated up inside to an unbearable temperature. The other Travelers turned and saw he was uncloaked and pale, with sweat pouring down his face. This should not have been so— since it was Winter Solstice—and while it wasn't like their winters back home, it was still cold.

No; Matt should not have been uncloaked and sweating.

With no warning, Miriam ripped her cloak off as well, revealing herself. She pressed her fingers to Matt's lips and screamed in a voice he'd never heard before now. It was deep and dark and certainly not the voice Miriam usually spoke with. For a second, he thought her eyes lost all color, but no, that couldn't be ... could it?

"You will say no more words!" she shrieked before turning to flee the group of shocked Travelers.

Matt fell to the ground, writhing in unbearable pain; the spot where that wretched girl had pierced his arm had greatly swollen up, forcing Matt to his knees. It was the same spot where she'd touched him back in the cave. Bella grabbed his arm and looked closely at it. It seemed unthinkable that just by grabbing his arm through a heavy cloak, one could do such damage.

"I cannot believe that louse is your cousin, Pierce!" Bella stated. "She is dreadful! Look at his arm!" she continued to shriek, holding it up for the others to see. Before any of their eyes could turn toward Matt's arm, however, something else demanded their attention. A great shout forced its way from Jennifer's belly out into the air that continued to swirl and twist around them.

"LOOK THERE ... AT THE SHORE!" she screamed.
Before anyone could say anything, Pierce, Sam, and Judah all dropped their cloaks and ran toward the sea. While they had been preoccupied with Matt's arm, Miriam had stolen his cloak and was now standing at the edge of the sea with the basket of clay tablets hooked over her arm.

"NO!" one shouted.

"GET HER!" screamed another.

They ran as fast as they had ever run before, but the girls who were still standing with Matt feared it would not be fast enough. Miriam had both hands filled with tablets with her right arm raised to throw them into the sea.

"MIRIAM," Pierce shouted. "STOP NOW!"

She lowered her arm and turned to face the ones running at her. She glared a piercing glare that shot right through the boys who were running.

"No. YOU stop," she demanded. "If you come one step more, this whole basket will be thrown into the sea, and all your precious tablets will be destroyed!" They stopped straightaway and moved no muscle. They knew this girl was outrageous enough to do what she had threatened.

"Miriam," Pierce begged. "Why would you destroy the tablets? Why don't you want to free Peter?"

She didn't care to take the time to respond, but just for the fun of it, she did.

"Because Peter is the only other one who knows what really happened. He knows you didn't push him in front of the car so I can't let him be freed from the curse … I just can't. The truth has to die with Peter."

That seemed like a selfish and shallow reason to keep a person's soul cursed, the Travelers thought. There had to be more to it than that. Surely, if Miriam's lie was found out, it could be forgiven, but clearly, Miriam did not want forgiveness. She wanted something more. She wanted power. She wanted a throne.

Miriam thought about trying to explain it all but decided against it. The more time she took with these Travelers, the more time it would take for her to get that throne she so desperately desired.

"But Miriam," Pierce wailed. He didn't understand that there was so much more behind her choice to destroy the tablets, not that it would have made any more sense to him if he did know all his cousin's reasonings. But to destroy the one thing that would free thousands of souls from a curse, just to keep her secret safe? That seemed unthinkable, and neither Pierce nor the others could make sense of it.

"I warned you, Pierce," Miriam screamed. She lifted her arm back up, ready to throw a number of the tablets into the sea. "I warned you not to return to Trilleah a long time ago, but you refused to listen. Do you remember?"

Pierce may not have remembered, but Bella did. The conversation she'd overheard in the dark passageway suddenly came back to her mind, and she remembered Miriam saying exactly that. Miriam was angry with Pierce for returning to Trilleah and had blamed him for her being there.

"Now I am telling you and everyone, get out of this land and get out now. You will not free anyone's souls here, not even one. Not now—not ever!"

"Jennifer," she seethed, "your precious mamma will be forever lost. You have wasted your time here. Go home, or die in Trilleah. It's your choice to make ..."

While everyone was listening intently to the words she was rambling on about, their eyes were on the tablets in her hands. Matt wanted to scream out, but his tongue had been silenced. He wondered, if Miriam succeeded in destroying the tablets and the Travelers did leave Trilleah, would he be mute for the rest of his life? Or would her dreadful curse eventually wear off?

A stupid and selfish thing to wonder about, I know, he cried to his Shailma since Shura was the only one who could hear him now.

"What happened to you, Miriam?" Pierce shouted. He didn't care since the girl had completely worn out his patience, but he wanted to keep her talking. "As long as she's talking," he whispered to the others, "she's not throwing the tablets."

"Keep her talking, Pierce," Judah whispered. "We'll try and come up with a plan." Without moving, Sam and Judah whispered back and forth, trying to make any sense out of these happenings while Pierce kept Miriam busy shouting back and forth.

"Miriam," he hollered. "Please … let's talk about this …"

"There's nothing to talk about!" she screamed. "I did what I did, and now I've made my decision. King Shrailzhar has promised me a throne of my own. I will rule over the land if I destroy the tablets and that's exactly what I'm going to do."

"WHAT?" The Travelers all shouted at once. They were horrified at such a promise and even more outraged that Miriam believed it. There was no way the king would ever share his kingdom with anyone—certainly not with this wretched little girl.

Miriam had been caught in a trap altogether different than anything they could imagine, and she didn't even realize it. It appeared that it was too late to change her mind. Obviously, she believed the king's promise.

Jennifer had heard enough. This wicked one had burned her lips and her tongue had been cursed to silence on the matter. But now, she was determined that even if she could not speak about it, her legs were not cursed from carrying her to Miriam and her hands were not cursed from removing the tablets from the wretch's hands.

Simeon, be with me, Jennifer pleaded as she ran with all her might toward Miriam.

"NO Jennifer! DON'T," the Travelers screamed. They believed Miriam's threat of throwing the basket into the sea if anyone came toward her.

As Jennifer ran past the others, she heard the sweet, peaceful melody rising from Kaija Mae's lips. What a sound. It brought enough courage to Jennifer's heart to keep her feet moving … moving straight toward Miriam … the very one she had tried so hard to avoid.

FOR MAMMA, Jennifer screamed in her mind.

For Mamma, she heard Simeon reply.

Jennifer reached Miriam just as she turned and hurled the first of the tablets into the sea. It hit Leviathan square in the nose and although it was a very small piece of clay compared to the size of his nose, it caught his attention. He turned and laid his eyes on the one who had thrown it. Everyone froze except Miriam, since she had not yet realized that Leviathan had locked his glare on her. Jennifer stopped running and stepped back as far as she could from the girl who had enraged the sea demon.

Miriam threw the other tablet from her hand into the basket and picked up the entire thing to throw at Leviathan. She was given no opportunity, however, for as she looked up, she saw the sea demon was coming toward her. She turned to run, dropping the basket as she went.

The tablets flung this way and that, but thankfully they were on the shore and not sinking to the bottom of the sea.

Leviathan's massive head was swinging toward Miriam, and as she tried to duck, it caught her. That large chunk of razor-sharp glass —or whatever it was—protruding from the top of Leviathan's head sliced straight through her back as she tried to run.

Miriam slumped to the ground with a hard thud.

Up From the Sea

Nobody moved. Nobody inhaled and nobody exhaled. They didn't know if Leviathan would go after them next. They expected he would and could think of no reason why he wouldn't.

Without their cloaks, they were fully exposed to the wrath of this sea demon. He seemed only interested in Miriam, however, and as she lay in a growing pool of her own blood, Leviathan brought his head down to her body and picked her up in his jaws. The Travelers were horrified! They didn't like the wretched girl, but none of them had ever wished her demise; at least, not like this.

The Travelers couldn't watch. Most looked away, certain that Leviathan would crunch her bones and easily devour her. As angry as they were with Miriam, nobody wanted this to be her end; it was far too gruesome to be the end of anyone. None wanted to watch as Miriam came to the end of herself.

Jennifer turned her eyes back to the tablets that were sprawled along the shore. Wave after wave was crashing hard on them, and she was terribly afraid they would be washed out to sea.

Pierce was the only one who kept a close watch on Leviathan because after all, no matter what she'd done or how evil Miriam's heart had become or what ridiculous covenants she'd made with King Shrailzhar, Miriam was, after all, his cousin. He felt responsible for her being in Trilleah in the first place. She was right, he supposed. If he had stayed away from the Dark Land, she would never have had to come and make sure her lies stayed hidden. It was too late to change any of the past, and as Pierce kept his eyes on Leviathan, he was surprised to see that the sea demon did not crunch her bones, nor did he swallow her up.

Instead, he swung his head far around one way and then flung it hard the other, throwing Miriam into the midst of the sea. And with that, Leviathan slid down slowly, slowly, slowly, until the last glimpse of the very top of his head disappeared beneath the water. He was gone.

"A wicked heart such as that one belongs to the sea," Matt said. Pierce heard him and even though Matt's words deeply saddened him, he knew they were correct. Wicked hearts did, in fact, belong in the depths of the sea. A wicked heart can never be trusted.

Matt began jumping for joy that the words he'd formed in his mouth rolled off of his tongue. He was worried they wouldn't; worried that with Miriam gone, the curse she'd put on him and Jennifer would remain forever.

He reached over and felt his arm. The wounds were gone. Every curse she'd put on them had vanished. It seemed that when Leviathan sliced through Miriam, all the curses she'd sent out were called back to rest upon her own soul.

There was much rejoicing that she was gone until Bella reminded them all that Miriam had managed to throw one tablet into the sea before Leviathan destroyed the wicked girl. The rejoicing ended abruptly. There was no use finding the last tablets if the first one had been destroyed. The entire dozen was required if the curse of the Waiting Ones was to be broken.

"What do we do now?" Jennifer sulked. She was the only one who'd gone over to pick up the scattered tablets. Two had been broken this morning when they left Asphelia's Hollow, but all the pieces were there—covered by the crud that the sea had washed in.

She shook the basket clean before carefully, and with teary eyes, laying the remaining tablets inside. As Jennifer would find one, she'd gently wipe it on her sleeve and run her fingers over the words. Then, with much care, the tablet would be set inside the basket.

One, after another, after another, she repeated this process until finally, Bella came to help. Matt soon joined them and then Kaija Mae. Slowly but surely, every Traveler—except for Pierce since he was greatly troubled—came over to the shore to help Jennifer dig through the sea crud and find the remaining tablets.

"Well," Kaija Mae finally said. "Looks like they're all here … except for that one."

"We need that one too, though," Jennifer whined. "There's no use looking for the last tablets now …"

With the tablets safely in the basket once more, the Travelers went back to retrieve their cloaks. They were empty of thought and heavy of heart. It appeared that all their journeys, the dangers they had gone through and the battles they had fought, were for no reason after all. A waste of time. The Waiting ones would remain cursed.

Jennifer could not make herself leave the shore, so she stayed. Surely there was no hurry now since the land was quiet and the gates were broken. She was in no hurry to leave and feared that once she left Trilleah, it would be for good. Her mamma's soul would remain under the curse of the Trows for all eternity, and King Shrailzhar would be victorious after all. She didn't want to leave Trilleah because she would be leaving Mamma behind for good.

Pierce saw her weeping and even though his own heart was heavy with despair, he felt saddened for the young girl who'd endured so much. After all, while Jennifer's thoughts were focused only on her mamma in the adder's pit, everyone else had been thinking of their own loved ones when she had been pulled beneath the ground. Pierce was no different, and as he looked at Jennifer weeping in the sludge of the seashore, he knew full well that every sacrifice she had made, was made for Peter, Justice, Tom and the others—as much as it was for her own mamma.

"Thank you," he said as he slumped on the shore beside the weeping girl. He had startled her, and she jolted upright and wiped her eyes.

"For what?" she asked, sniffling between her words.

"Everything! Jennifer, we almost did it. YOU almost did it."

She wanted to keep right on sobbing, but there was something in Pierce's words that wouldn't let her. He put his arm around the frail, worn-out little girl. She laid her head on his shoulder and wept. He said nothing but leaned his head down until it was touching hers and wept right along with her.

As the most unlikely pair sat on the shore wailing and sobbing together, the most miraculous of all miraculous things ever to happen in the history of miraculous things, happened.

Something smacked Jennifer on the foot. She would never have felt it since the boots that normally covered her feet were thick. But as it was, she had run clean out of her boots when she was coming after Miriam, so her feet were bare and whatever had hit her, was felt.

She looked down through her tears. Jennifer wiped her eyes and looked down again. Then something else hit her foot. Her stomach churned, and she feared she'd throw up on Pierce, so she moved away a little.

"NO," she whispered in disbelief.

"What?" Pierce asked, wiping his own eyes and looking over at her.

"Look … there by my feet," she whispered again, afraid to speak too loudly in case she was not seeing correctly what had been thrown out of the sea by the crashing waves.

Pierce's eyes slowly moved toward Jennifer's feet. As he caught sight of what she'd seen—what she'd felt bump into her foot—he jumped. Oh, how he jumped.

The boy who was normally grumpy and sullen now danced around like a drunken sailor and sang. He was a terrible singer. He started singing and dancing and throwing his hands up into the air. Pierce bent down and picked up Jennifer, and together they danced all over the seashore.

The other Travelers who had been sitting a long way back by the cloaks, watching the two weep together, were surprised at such a shift in the two's actions. They jumped up and ran back down to the shore to see what had caused such excitement.

"What's going on?" Bella hollered.

"Have you finally gone mad?" Kaija Mae demanded of them. She was completely serious and waited for an answer.

"Not at all!" Pierce shouted.

"Then what it is?" Sam asked again. They were getting annoyed because something wonderful had obviously happened and they wanted to know what it was. The two who were dancing on the shore didn't seem to be able to pull themselves away from jumping and squealing long enough to say what that something wonderful was, though.

"Did you come up with a plan?" Judah asked.

"Nope," Jennifer laughed.

"Then WHAT?" Sam demanded.

Finally, the two calmed down enough to point to the shore and scream.

"LOOK!" Jennifer wailed.

"SEE THERE!" Pierce hooted and hollered.

Judah went to where they were pointing and squatted down to get a closer look. He bent over and put his hand under a bit of crud from the sea and pulled out …

A TABLET!

The very tablet that Miriam had thrown into the sea had been thrown right back to the Travelers. The enormous waves continued to crash down, soaking Judah, but he didn't notice. What he did notice, however, close to the tablet he'd just picked out of the sludge, was something that looked just like the tablet in his hand.

"It couldn't be," he said to himself. But oh, it was indeed. Matt shoved his hand into the crud once again and pulled out a second tablet.

The sea, the very thing they thought was going to be the end of their journey, had delivered right into their hands a clay tablet. Matt held one tablet in one hand and a second tablet in his other. Oh, he held them tightly. He lifted those tablets high into the air and shouted. The rest of the Travelers began shouting as well, and for the very longest time, the Travelers danced and sang and shouted and whooped and hollered.

They were no longer afraid of Leviathan. It seemed he had done what he'd needed to do and had gone back to his home under the sea. They were not afraid of the Army of Shrailzhar who seemed to have returned to the forest. After all, guarding Malleana forest was their main assignment and they had already wandered much too far from it.

And then they cried. Each one, in turn, slid to the ground and sobbed. The journey they thought was over was far from it. The cursed souls were close to being freed and the thought of such great freedom brought the Travelers to their knees, weeping.

For a long time they went from rejoicing to quietness to weeping and around and around and around again. It made no difference that the sun had set hours ago because the gates had been broken down, never to close again. The Travelers could no longer be trapped in its grip, and this too, caused rejoicing and weeping all at the same time. Their emotions were both heavy and light and they wore the Travelers out.

Finally, exhausted and likely unable to find their way back to Asphelia's Hollow in such darkness, they laid on their backs and listened to the waves lap softly at the shore. Oh, how they would have enjoyed looking at the stars or falling asleep under the moonlight—but not in Trilleah. In this dark and evil land, the stars had fallen from the sky long ago, they were sure, and the moon refused to share its light.

Suddenly and without any warning, the waves which had been calm rose up and smashed hard onto the Travelers. Leviathan leaped from the sea and with the smallest glimmer of light escaping from a few remaining burning shrubs, they saw just how enormous the beast was. The Travelers jumped to their feet and grabbed ahold of one another.

"RUN!" Pierce bellowed … and run they did.

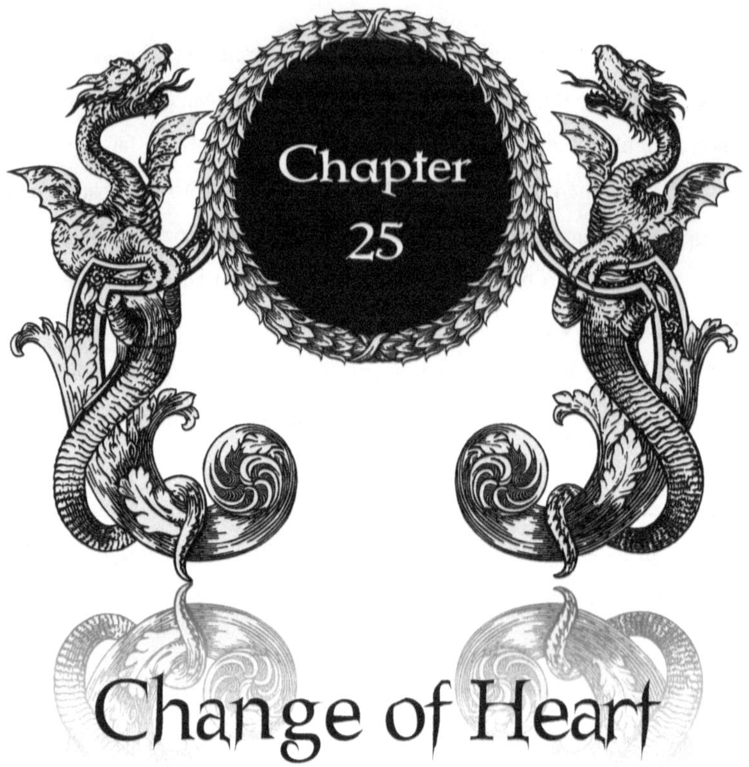

Chapter 25

Change of Heart

No matter where they ran, the land shook. It seemed King Shrailzhar had found out the sea had given up its tablet and he was enraged. The sea churned hard. Lightning came from the small rips in the sky, tearing them wide open, and pummeled the sea with bolts of torment. The burning shrubs stopped giving up their light, and the Travelers could see nothing when the lightning wasn't being thrown down.

They could hear, though. They heard Leviathan shrieking and howling, and the Travelers were almost glad they couldn't see since they knew the lightning was aimed—and being thrown—at the sea demon.

Yes, King Shrailzhar was tremendously furious. His precious Miriam had been done away with and now he had no one to destroy the clay tablets. The wretched king knew the end of his kingdom was near; he had no choice but to destroy it. Trilleah was being torn apart and was destroying itself and the Travelers had to get out. Somehow, they had to get out of this dark and dreadful land immediately. All hope of finding the remaining tablet vanished.

"WHO HAS THE TABLETS?" Judah hollered.

"I DO," Pierce shouted back.

It was hard to hear one another since the winds had risen and were now howling dreadfully loud. They were so intense that it felt as if the Travelers were being pulled into the twisting of a tornado.

"Hold on to each other," Bella screamed. They moved closer together and clung to one another with all their might.

Jennifer and Pierce had no time to put their cloaks on and had been carrying them instead. But a nasty wind had come and swiped them both, throwing them high into the sky. Now those two Travelers were fully uncovered and would remain that way.

Oh, how they wanted to run, but even standing upright had become a challenge. As the land shook and twisted itself, large chunks of the ground were being violently ripped up. Whatever was below the ground was giving off a small glimmer of light, and the Travelers were briefly grateful. Not much light snuck out, but enough that they could see a little bit here, and a wee bit there.

If only the Travelers could have known that what was just beneath them—separated by only a measly layer of ground—was a horrendous and bubbling sea of liquid fire they would not have been grateful at all. That fire was what was giving a sliver of light, but if the Travelers would have known, they'd have gladly chosen to remain in the dark.

Kaija Mae was singing her songs, but nobody could hear them. It made no difference to her; it was not for the other Travelers that she sang. It never was.

"OVER THERE," Judah shouted. He pulled and tugged as they were going against the vicious winds and tried desperately to get to a cave that he'd spotted. It might not be the safest place, but then again, there were no safe places in this land; not anymore. There were no bugs, no serpents or vipers, no armies, and no King Shrailzhar riding on his hideous beast. They too had all taken shelter. This cave was the only shelter the Travelers could find, and so it would have to do.

They finally worked their way to the opening of the cave and without even thinking to check it out first, they ducked inside and fell to the ground, exhausted.

"What are we going to do?" Jennifer wailed. Indeed, this journey had taken its toll on her and she felt like she was going to break into a million pieces. "How are we going to find the way back to the hollow?"

"I honestly don't know," Bella cried. "I know I always have an answer and sometimes, even when I don't have one—I make one up. But now," she waved her hands directing all their attention to the crumbling walls of the cave, "I don't have an answer, even a made-up one."

They laid on the ground, hoping it would not crumble beneath them. They watched the rock ceiling and prayed it wouldn't fall on top of them and crush them. They kept an eye on the walls and crossed their fingers that they wouldn't crumble so much that they collapsed, burying the Travelers alive.

This was not where they wanted to be, but it was where they were.

"I think," Judah said, "we need to stay hidden in here for the night—or until the sun comes up—and then try and make our way back to Asphelia's Hollow as soon as there's enough light to see the way."

Nobody spoke because nobody wanted to agree with him, although they knew he had suggested the only reasonable suggestion.

Finally, Pierce agreed. "I think that's our only choice," he said. "It sounds like the winds are calming a little but not nearly enough to go wandering around Trilleah in the dark."

"Then it's decided," Bella announced. "We shall stay here for the night."

Kaija Mae again began her singing, and it brought a slight—a very slight—calm to the cave.

"I wish we brought more food," Jennifer said just as her belly growled. They all agreed.

Shortly, the winds outside the cave had died down completely, and the Travelers could hear Leviathan screaming as the lightning continued to be thrown down, striking him repeatedly. Without a doubt, the king blamed the sea demon for returning the lost tablet and also for releasing the eleventh tablet to the Travelers.

As the night slowly dragged on, the winds picked up and died down—over and over, throughout most of the night. Leviathan continued to scream and throw out hideous wails. Rocks crumbled here and there, and the ground rumbled beneath them continuously. It was going to be a long night.

"If we can get back to the hollow in the morning—if it's still standing—we'll be able to find some food and the maps to lead us to the last tablet," Pierce said. For the first time, he realized the curse of the Trows might actually be broken, and Malleana Forest might finally be forced to give up the souls of the Waiting Ones.

His attitude toward the Travelers had changed considerably over the last few hours, and instead of being his usual nasty self, he was surprisingly kind and compassionate. Pierce realized that without Jennifer, they would never have found as many of the tablets as they had. It was her who had gone to the most horrible of places to retrieve them. It was Jennifer who'd gone down into the adder's pit, and Jennifer who had to fight the vipers and the dragons … and the king.

Also, he was being more sweet and protective of Bella than ever before, and even now, as they shivered under their cloaks in the damp darkness of the cave, Pierce had moved close to her. He was without a cloak, and Bella was genuinely glad to be able to share hers with the boy.

"Jennifer," he called. "Come over here—by me."

She thought it odd but did what he asked. For the first time since she'd arrived at Trilleah, she felt safe with Pierce, as though he wanted to protect her rather than annoy her and truly, he did.

Pierce suddenly had an eery knowing that if they were to find the last tablet, and that was a big if, that Jennifer would need to be kept safe. He wondered if the maps would be able to direct them at all now that the land had been shaken so badly that nothing was where it was supposed to be. He kept all his wonderings buried in his mind, though, since he did not want to upset the others any more than they already were. Of course, they were all wondering the same things, but since none of them voiced the fearful thoughts, nobody knew that they were all thinking the same thoughts.

As Pierce wondered about Jennifer, he heard the voice of his Shailma. He was not especially familiar with it, and he never listened too carefully to the voice when he did hear it. Often, he ignored it all together. This time he paid close attention because he'd watched Jennifer and Judah listen and obey their Shailmas many times and he had seen the effects of it. Certainly, if the twins had not listened to their Shailmas and followed their direction, none of them would be here now, and the clay tablets would have never been collected.

Nothing is ever as it should be, his Shailma whispered to him.

And then, in the next few words, suddenly everything made sense to him. The last words he heard his Shailma whisper before Pierce drifted into a restless sleep, were the same words that Jennifer's Shailma had told her time and time again.

But everything is as it must be.

And indeed, everything was … for now.

… UNTIL THE NEXT JOURNEY …

Mist Over Leviathan

The Beyond Solstice Gates Series:

1. Casting Shadows

> Where truth exists ... even if no one believes it.

2. The Fowler's Snare

> Strength is found when the eye sees
> what the heart already knows.

3. Perfidy of Labyrinth

> Where the only way forward is all the way back.

4. Veiled Sun ✧ Blood Moon

> Where the sun gives no light and the moon throws great
> drops of blood ... singing of both a great and terrible day.

5. Mist Over Leviathan

> Where wickedness of the heart is revealed and
> thrown into the depths of the sea.

6. War of the Firmament

> Where what lies above and what lies beneath,
> is nothing compared to what lies within.

7. Chasm of Acheron